The Valiant King

The Fallen King Chronicles Book 3

RICHARD FIERCE

ebook ISBN: 978-1-947329-17-1
Print ISBN-13: 978-1-947329-18-8

CONTENTS

RICHARD FIERCE

ACKNOWLEDGMENTS

To my amazing wife. May this book not bring you as much emotional turmoil as the last one.

—Garrick

CHAPTER 1

A light breeze blew in from the east, causing Garrick's cloak to stir slightly. He closed his eyes and breathed the cool air in deep then exhaled slowly. He opened his eyes and saw the sun was just beginning to rise, bathing the dark sky in soothing reds and pinks. The beauty of the heavens was almost enough to forget reality.

Almost.

Garrick turned his gaze to the fields outside the castle. As far as he could see, makeshift tents blotted out the scenery. Here and there he could pick out movement among the camp as they slowly awakened.

He considered, as he had many times since their arrival, why they were here. Thousands of them, slowly encroaching into his kingdom. From the corner of his eye, he noticed one of his scouts approaching.

"My Lord," the man said as he drew near before dropping down on one knee.

"Please rise," Garrick answered, turning away from the elvish army. "What do you have to report?"

"Their numbers are growing. More elves show up every day. We haven't been able to get close enough to find their leader's tent yet, but we are working on it. It's not easy to slip past their guards. Magic and whatnot."

Garrick nodded. "I understand. Do the best you can. That's all I ask." He turned back to the fields. After a few moments, he realized the man was still standing there. He turned to him, raising his eyebrows questioningly.

"You didn't dismiss me, my Lord."

"My apologies," Garrick replied. He nodded toward the elvish army. "Why do you suppose they are here?"

The scout shrugged. "I'm not sure. Perhaps they want their land back."

"Excuse me?"

"You know, from the old stories? Supposedly the elves lived in these lands before humans pushed them into the desert. Maybe they want their land back." The man shrugged again.

"It's definitely something to consider," Garrick said. "Thank you. You are dismissed." The man bowed low and left.

Garrick rubbed his chin as he considered what the scout said. Perhaps the man was right. It had been a long time since he had heard those stories of history. Was there truth to them? He didn't know. He would definitely need to research it.

An explosion shook the ground beneath his feet.

"And so it begins again," he muttered. It had been two weeks since he arrived, bringing fresh reinforcements to help stem the tide of elves overrunning his cities. They were using their strange magic to create holes in the walled cities, enabling their warriors to storm through and massacre his people.

After three cities had fallen, he mustered as many men as he could and made his way to the battlefront.

He'd sent runners to the outer cities, calling on his generals and their men to follow suit. They were slowly starting to arrive.

Once he had witnessed how the elves were getting through the defenses of his cities, he had placed archers on the walls and ordered them to cut down the elves rushing the walls.

And it had worked. The elves finally stopped trying to breach the walls. The last two days had essentially been a stalemate with neither side attacking the other. Garrick ran to where a group of soldiers had gathered.

"What's happening?" he asked.

"One of them rushed the wall, but Tarn here shot him down right before he hit it."

"Excellent job, Tarn. Was it just the one?"

"Yes, sir."

"They're testing us, probably to see if we are still paying attention," Garrick said.

"That's what we were thinking, sir."

"Keep me posted. If anything happens, I want to be alerted immediately."

"Will do, sir."

Garrick left the wall and headed down the steps, walking toward the main keep. The generals who had arrived late last night were supposed to be gathering there now. A messenger waved him over.

"There's a battalion roughly a mile out," he said breathlessly.

"I appreciate the update," Garrick said. The messenger sprinted off, likely to deliver more news elsewhere.

He entered the keep and made his way to the appointed room. Silence ensued and everyone in the room bowed as he entered.

"Thank you for making haste," Garrick said. "Please be seated." After everyone had found a seat, he also took a seat and then briefed them on the current situation.

"What has brought them to our doorstep?" Rycroft, one of the generals, asked.

"That is the question, isn't it?" Garrick motioned to one of the guards standing nearby. The man came over and unrolled a map that was on the table. He placed four small stones onto the map, one at each corner.

"This is a map of the area. Our position is marked with the green square here," Garrick pointed to a spot on the map.

"Our enemy encampment is here in red. The last two days have been silent. Before that, they had men rushing the walls and using their magic to blow holes in the stone. Our archers put a stop to that."

He ran his finger from the enemy camp north to the Deadlands. "This is the route they are taking to arrive here. Every day more of them turn up. The curious thing is that they are all men."

"What do you mean?"

Garrick looked to Rycroft. The man was intelligent when it came to tactics on the battlefield. He was one of the few who had given him a run for his gold when he was working to unify the generals. It seemed so long ago, but only a few months had passed since Garrick was crowned king.

"They are all men. No women or children are among the camps. Curious, is it not?" Some of the generals muttered to themselves.

"Where do you suppose they are?" Garrick asked.

"Perhaps they are still in the Deadlands?" again, Rycroft answered.

"Perhaps. Assuming they are, who do you suppose is protecting them?"

Again, murmurs filled the room.

"If all of their warriors are coming here, it seems likely there is no one protecting their women and children. Which opens a possibility of us ending this battle, or at the very least, postponing it long enough for us to rally more soldiers here."

"What are you suggesting?" Caidan, one of the younger men, asked.

Garrick rose from his chair and clasped his hands behind his back. His eyes looked from one general to the next, moving around the table and finally stopping at Rycroft.

"I am suggesting that we send a contingent of men into the Deadlands to find their women and children."

Instead of the murmuring, there was only silence. "Make no mistake, I am not proposing that we massacre them. We are not barbarians. But I believe if we can find them, we can use them to our advantage."

Caidan ran his left hand over his bearded face. "What's the plan, then?"

"I need a volunteer to take a few men and follow the route the elves are coming from. You'll need to act as scouts. Follow the trail and find their source, or at the very least one of their camps. Ensure there are women and children, then send one of the men back here with the location. I'll dispatch soldiers during the night and the scout will lead them to the camp."

"What then?" Rycroft asked.

"Then, depending on the situation here, we'll decide what our next move is. I understand you'll all need time to think it over. Take the rest of the day and sleep on it. I'll need to know who is volunteering by tomorrow at first light. Are there any questions?"

"Yes," Caidan said. "We know their men have magical tattoos. What of their women? Do they have them as well?"

"That we are unsure of," Garrick answered. "I have scribes searching every library for information on our enemy. That is one of the questions I am looking to have answered."

"What other information are you looking for?"

"I am looking for the truth," Garrick said. "I'm sure you all know the stories."

"What stories are you referring to? Their magical prowess? Their deadly homeland? Their—"

"Where they originated from," Garrick interrupted Caidan. "I'm talking about the stories of where they came from. There are some stories that say parts of Talvaard and parts of Oakvalor used to be home to the elves until humans pushed them into the desert."

"Those are childish fairy tales," Caidan scoffed. "They're used to scare children into obedience." His next words were said with a mocking tone: "'Do as you are told so the elves don't come for you and drag you off into the Deadlands as punishment for their banishment.'"

"Perhaps you are right," Garrick replied. "And perhaps you are wrong. We don't know if they are fairy tales or if they are historical truths. Until we do, I suggest everyone keep an open mind. Suppose it is true. Suppose that our ancestors did indeed push them into the desert. Why do you think they would be here, after all this time, attacking our cities?"

"Revenge?" Rycroft suggested.

"Precisely. What if they have come to take their land back?"

"That's preposterous!" Caidan barked.

"Is it?" Garrick asked.

"You're serious?" Caidan said, seeming to realize that Garrick was posing a genuine theory.

"Absolutely. Keep an open mind. Your people are pushed from their homes. They are possibly struggling to survive in a foreign land. Eventually, they grow in strength and they are constantly reminded of what happened to them. What do you think it would lead to?"

"I suppose it's possible," Caidan confessed

hesitantly.

"That's all I'm suggesting," Garrick replied. "That it is possible the stories are true. And if they are, I don't see this being a short battle."

"You think this will turn into a siege?" Caidan asked.

"No. They will not stop until they succeed. I am sure this will turn into a war."

The generals exchanged looks.

"That's all I have for now," Garrick waved dismissively. "I ask that you all meet here again in the morning. Until then, see to your men and get what rest you can. Dismissed."

Garrick turned and left the room, likely leaving his generals confused. He tried not to let it bother him. He was just as confused about the motive of the elves himself.

He noticed soldiers running toward the northern wall. Shouting filled the air. He stopped one of the men running by.

"What's going on?" he demanded.

"The elves, my Lord! They're rushing the walls again!"

Garrick dismissed the man with a nod and ran toward the stairs leading to the battlements. He bounded up the stairs two at a time and rushed to the wall. Down below, a group of elves were running toward the castle.

Arrows whistled through the air, some striking the ground around them. A few of them hit their mark and the elves staggered and tumbled to the ground. Caidan and Rycroft came and stood on either side of him, watching the spectacle.

"I thought they stopped attacking the walls with the archers up here?" Caidan asked.

"They did," Garrick answered. "I don't understand this foolish move."

The remaining elves stopped their approach and

began lifting their fallen comrades. Garrick assumed they were going to remove their bodies from the battlefield. Instead, the elves used the bodies as shields and continued their trek toward the castle.

"Take them down!" Garrick shouted.

More arrows filled the air. The few elves remaining were quickly killed and a cheer roused from the archers. Garrick watched the encampment. There was no reason to celebrate.

The elves had proven somewhat intelligent in their attacks against the walls. It seemed out of place for them to attack now, knowing their warriors were at the mercy of his bowmen. An unsettling feeling crept into his stomach.

"Something's not right," he muttered.

"What's that?" Rycroft asked.

"Something's not right. They wouldn't attack like this. Not with the archers up here." His mind began racing through scenarios. He looked toward the archers and whistled. One of them jogged over.

"Captain, have some men sweep the walls. Tell them to keep their eyes sharp."

The man nodded and left, his pace much faster than before.

"What do you think they're doing?" Caidan asked.

"I'm not sure, but I think they're creating a diversion."

As if to prove him right, a horn sounded from the eastern side of the castle. Garrick sprinted in that direction, Caidan and Rycroft following close behind him.

Before they were halfway there, an explosion sounded and the castle walls shook violently. Garrick leaned up against the outer wall to keep his balance.

"They've hit the wall!" he shouted.

As soon as the shaking settled, he stood up straight

and continued running to where a crowd of archers had gathered. He reached the area just as they let off a volley of arrows. Garrick looked down to see a charred spot on the wall and the body of an elf lying nearby.

"He got right up to the wall before we knew he was even approaching," one of the bowmen said. "We hit him right before he made it."

Garrick saw a small group of elves approaching slowly. "There," he said, pointing to their position.

"They're out of range, but we'll hit them hard as soon as they get close."

Garrick nodded and watched their advance. "Why aren't they running?" he asked to no one in particular.

"What do you mean?" Caidan asked.

"They normally rush the walls. Why are they walking?"

Everyone remained silent. After what seemed like an eternity, Garrick heard the captain shout an order.

A stream of arrows whistled through the air. Garrick squinted his eyes, thinking he was seeing things. It looked as though the arrows had bounced off the elves.

"What happened?" he asked.

"I'm not sure," Rycroft said uncertainly, also squinting into the distance.

"Draw!" The captain shouted beside him. The archers knocked their arrows to their bowstrings and pulled the strings back.

"Loose!"

Another torrent of arrows showered down among the elves. They were still too far away to be certain, but Garrick again thought the arrows had fallen harmlessly off them.

"Someone get me a spyglass," Garrick ordered. A moment later the Captain handed him one. Garrick pulled on the end of the spyglass, extending it as far as it would go, then placed it to his eye and located the elves.

"Draw! Loose!"

He watched carefully as the arrows descended upon them. This time, there was no mistaking it. The arrows *were* bouncing off them.

"Impossible," he breathed.

"What is it?" Caidan asked. "What's happening?"

Garrick handed him the instrument. "The arrows … they're, they're ineffective," he said, not wanting to say it aloud. Caidan used the spyglass and watched as another volley of arrows filled the air.

"By the Divines," Caidan whispered in awe. "They're bouncing right off them!"

"Draw! Loose!" the Captain shouted again.

Garrick considered telling them to hold their arrows, but he wasn't sure if that was the right decision. If it were some sort of spell, would it eventually wear off as the arrows continued to hit their invisible shield? He looked to the captain and could tell he was thinking the same thing.

"Keep firing," Garrick commanded. The captain nodded.

"What does this mean?" Caidan asked. "I've never seen anything like this."

"Neither have I," Rycroft chimed in.

Garrick remained mute. He didn't know what it meant, and he didn't like it. The tattoo on his forearm began to itch. Subconsciously he rubbed at it. It was covered by a thin piece of material that looked like his skin and was held in place with sticky resin. Besides that, it was hidden beneath the sleeve of his shirt.

What is this threat, Mordum? He prayed mentally. He glanced at his generals from the corner of his eyes. No one knew he was a follower of Mordum. Not a single soul. Not even his wife knew. He despised keeping secrets from her, but this was different. This could destroy everything he had worked to build and protect.

He turned his attention back to the elves. They were much closer. He didn't need the spyglass now to see that the arrows had no effect. He watched as the arrows struck the elves innocently and then fell to the ground like twigs.

They looked different from the other elves. There was something odd about their skin color. Garrick frowned as he studied them.

And then he realized the danger. Located in the center of the group of elves, hunched down and hidden by their odd skinned brethren, were more elves. Just like the others who rushed the walls. His eyes widened in understanding.

"Captain, in the center! Aim for the center of the group!"

The captain looked intently at the elves and then snapped his gaze to Garrick, the fear evident in his eyes.

Garrick pointed toward the elves. "Aim for the center, Captain!"

The man shook his head as if waking from a dream and started directing the bowmen. Arrows filled the air again, raining down among the elves. Garrick began formulating plans if they should break through the wall.

Once the wall was compromised, it would be hard to keep them out. He had read the reports from the previous city that had fallen. The elves would throw themselves into a group of soldiers and use their explosive magic to destroy men as easily as they destroyed stone.

He turned to Caidan and Rycroft. "If they break through the walls, we have to do everything we can to hold them off. Seal the hole if possible." His generals nodded their understanding.

The wall shook as an explosion rocked the ground below. Garrick and his generals pressed themselves up against the wall. Several more explosions went off and the wall shuddered intensely. The Captain was still directing the bowmen.

Garrick waited a few moments before looking over the wall again. Several of the elves lay dead, full of arrows. The odd skinned ones began stacking the bodies up against the wall. He watched as the arrows continued to assail them, all to no good. They continued to bounce off harmlessly.

A horn sounded from the north. Before Garrick could turn his attention that way, hundreds of elves suddenly came into view. They were sprinting across the field toward the wall. He looked about frantically, trying to figure out what they were doing.

He looked back down at the elves stacking bodies. Realization dawned on him. With no time to shout a warning, he watched in horror as one of the elves leaped through the air toward the pile of bodies.

A brilliant light blinded him. Garrick's eyes watered up as an explosion jolted the wall, much harder than the others. He lost his footing and fell to the hard stone. He blinked his eyes rapidly, trying to clear his vision. Rycroft was standing over him.

"Are you all right?"

Garrick nodded. He accepted Rycroft's arm and stood up. Shouting erupted below and Garrick realized the elves had blown a hole in the wall. He looked over the wall's edge and saw hundreds of elves running toward the breach. He knew what he had to do. He considered alternative options, but he knew none of them were guaranteed to work. They had to close the opening and seal the hole.

He turned to Rycroft and Caidan. "You two are in charge. Do your best to keep them from overtaking the castle. If it comes down to it, pull back and regroup at the closest city on this route. That's likely their next target. There's a battalion less than a mile out. Make sure they know to divert there as well."

"What are talking about?" Rycroft asked.

"Just do as I command," Garrick answered sternly. "We don't have time to debate."

"Yes, my Lord." Rycroft looked questioningly at him.

"What is it?" Garrick asked.

"What are you going to do?"

Garrick clenched his jaw. "I'm going to crush them."

He climbed atop the wall and watched as the mass of elves coalesced on the breach. He looked back to Rycroft and Caidan, nodded once, then leaped off the wall.

"Greatness is reached through perseverance."

—Jerik

CHAPTER 2

Release me.

Aramis startled awake, kicking off the thin piece of cloth that served as a blanket. Though his prison cell was dark and cold, his skin was burning and he was covered in sweat. Ever since he tapped into the power of the tattoo, it seemed as though his visions were more real.

"Another nightmare?"

The voice came from the cell across from his. Aramis didn't bother responding. He didn't know who was also being held prisoner, and he didn't care. He just wanted out.

Sitting upon the stone slab that was his bed, he rubbed his hands over his face. He considered how the Prophet of Edria, the leader of Mel's order, had betrayed him. He shook his head, knowing Mel would have been crushed by it.

"Oh Mel," he sighed, thinking of his friend. The man had willingly stayed behind to face a templar of Mordum in order to save Aramis's life. A sacrifice, it seemed, made in vain by the Prophet's treachery.

Grinding his teeth in frustration, he began pacing his cell. It wasn't very large. He guessed it to be six feet wide and ten feet long.

And it was always cold. He figured the dungeon must be underground because the walls and floor were cool to the touch and there were no windows. He couldn't tell if it was day or night. The little bit of light available belonged to a single torch a few cells down. It illuminated almost nothing, but Aramis had quickly realized it wasn't meant for the prisoners.

Eventually, he stopped his pacing and sat on the floor, leaning his back against the wall. He yawned and pondered how many days he had been locked in the cell. His thoughts wandered to how his people were faring. The nobles had always relied so heavily on his father.

From his conversation with Lord Bavol, the nobles seemed divided on their loyalty to this new king. Aramis still didn't believe the man was his brother. He would need a lot more proof than the word of a blind seer and the whispers of the court.

A scratching noise drew his attention. He held his breath and listened intently. It was coming from the edge of his cell. Rising slowly, he stepped over to his bed and continued to listen. It was definitely coming from somewhere close.

He knelt down and crawled to the left corner of the cell. The scratching got louder. He thought at first it might be a rat, but as he felt around on the floor, his hand bumped something smooth.

Hesitantly, he felt around the smooth object and picked it up. He realized the scratching was coming from inside whatever he was holding. A soft cracking sound echoed in his cell. He dropped the thing as he felt it move in his hands. He wished he could see what it was. Looking at his arm to where he knew the tattoo of

Mordum was, he wondered if it would be any help.

Aramis had tried to use the tattoo to escape his cell shortly after being thrown into it, but nothing had happened. Other than his ability to run faster, he hadn't discovered any other powers from the mark.

He placed his fingers on the tattoo and closed his eyes, willing the tattoo to bless him with sight in the dark. Not sure if it worked or not, he opened his eyes and gasped slightly. It *had* worked! Somewhat, at least. He couldn't see perfectly, but he could see vague shapes.

The bed, the outline of the stones of the floor and walls, and the egg-shaped item that was moving. He squinted his eyes and leaned forward.

Suddenly a phiebus leaped at him. He shouted in surprise and scrambled back. The creature was quick and leaped on him, scratching and biting. Aramis used his hands to shield his face and rolled onto his stomach, trying to protect himself.

He lay there for a moment, waiting for the creature to jump on his back. Nothing happened. Rolling onto his side, he looked to where the phiebus was. Only it wasn't there. And neither was the egg. None of it was real. Aramis slowly got to his feet. Were the visions happening while he was awake now?

"Are you okay over there?"

It was the man in the cell across from him again. His first instinct was to continue to disregard the man. But if he was going to be here indefinitely, he might as well pass the time with someone.

"I'm fine," he answered.

"Ah, you can speak. I was beginning to wonder if you were mute until I heard you shouting."

"I'm not mute," Aramis smiled as he talked, "I was ignoring you."

The man laughed. "Ha! Honesty is my favorite attribute in men. I appreciate that."

Aramis laughed as well, the feeling of hopelessness fleeing momentarily. He tried to use the power of his tattoo to see the man, but that ability must have also been part of his vision, for it didn't work.

"So what did you do to get thrown down here?" the man asked.

"It's a long story," Aramis answered, not wanting to think about it.

"I don't know about you, but all I've got is time."

Aramis considered the man's words and knew he was right.

"I was betrayed," he said softly. Aramis started talking, telling the man everything he had been through the last few weeks. His father's murder, the man who tortured him thinking to get a confession of the murder, and the Prophet's betrayal. The more he talked about it, the less it stung.

"My friend Mel threw himself into the path of danger to let me get away. He was a loyal companion. A hero."

"Did he die?" the man asked.

"I'm sure he did. He stood against a powerful force."

"I'm sorry that you've gone through so much in such a short time."

"Thank you," Aramis said. "What about you? How did you end up down here?"

"I'm in exile," he replied. "And the Prophet didn't like what I had to say."

"Why are you in exile?"

"My homeland was attacked and I had to flee to survive."

"I didn't think you were from Oakvalor. You have an odd accent."

"No, I am not from Oakvalor. My home is far from here."

"I'm sorry you've lost your homeland. For what it's worth, if you make it out of here, I welcome you to

Oakvalor. You are more than welcome to build a new life here."

They continued talking until one of the priests brought food. Aramis's stomach growled and he realized he didn't know how long had passed since they fed him last. The priest was carrying a tray which he set down on the floor.

Grabbing a bowl off the tray, he then unlocked the cell door and kept Aramis at bay with a sword. He knelt down and placed the bowl on the floor inside the cell, keeping a wary eye on Aramis.

"I'm not going to do anything," Aramis said.

"I don't trust your words, vile scum of Mordum," the priest retorted as he closed the door and re-locked it. Picking up the tray, he left without another word.

Aramis picked up the bowl and sat on the edge of his bed. His mouth watered from his hunger. He raised the bowl to his lips and began to drink whatever was in it.

It was definitely watered down. A few pieces of what he assumed was meat were tough and hard to chew. He paused suddenly when he realized the guard had not given the other prisoner any food.

"Hey," he called out, pausing a moment when he realized he didn't know the man's name. "The guard didn't leave you anything, did he?"

"No," came the answer.

"Would you like to share mine?"

"I appreciate the offer, but no thank you."

"Are you sure?" Aramis asked. "I don't mind."

"I am sure," the man answered. Shrugging, Aramis finished off what remained and left the bowl by the door.

"What do they call you?" Aramis asked.

"My name is Tael. And yours?"

"Aramis," he answered. "It's nice to have someone to speak with."

"I agree," Tael said.

"I think I'm going to rest now," Aramis informed him.

"Enjoy," Tael replied.

"I'll try," Aramis laughed as he laid on the hard bed of stone.

● ∞ ● ∞ ●

Aramis slowly opened his eyes, waking for the first time from a sleep that was not riddled with nightmares. He sat up and noticed that the bowl he set by the door was gone. He didn't remember hearing the gate open. He must have been in a deep sleep. He stretched and began to perform his exercise routine. He did several sets of pushups and sit-ups, pushing himself until his muscles burned with the exertion.

"A fit body equates to a fit mind," as one of his father's generals always said. He didn't know when he might get out of the cell, but that didn't mean he shouldn't be ready when he did get out. He assumed Tael was sleeping, for the man wasn't trying to talk his ear off again.

The sound of footsteps caught his attention. Aramis stepped up to the bars of his cell and peered out. A group of priests was approaching. They stopped in front of his cell and one of them unlocked the door.

"The Prophet wants to see you," the one with the keys said.

Aramis shrugged and stepped out into the hall. The priests formed a circle around him and led him through the dungeon to the stairs that spiraled up into the main portion of the temple. As they climbed the stairs, Aramis's thought ran wild with what the Prophet might want. Regardless of what it was, he would refuse.

As they reached the door that led into the temple, the light blinded him. He stopped mid-step, shaking his head and blinking back the tears that overwhelmed his eyes. The priests didn't appreciate the abrupt stop and pushed him, causing him to fall onto the floor.

One of them kicked him several times in the side. He grunted under the force of the priest's blows and tried to block the kicks with his arm. Finally, the priest stopped and the others grabbed him, lifting him roughly onto his feet.

Aramis felt as though fire was burning inside his ribs. He gritted his teeth against the pain and tried to move at a pace that kept the priests from shoving him. They turned down a long hallway and he immediately knew where he was.

They stopped at the Prophet's door and led him inside. The room was the same as it was the first time he had been in it. There were no windows in the chamber, just several candles on the desk. And standing behind the desk was the traitor himself.

Aramis didn't bother to hide his hatred for the man. He glared openly at the Prophet. If his look bothered the man, he did well not to show it. He stood with his hands clasped behind his back. His black hair gleamed slightly in the light of the candles. The priests pushed Aramis forward until he was standing a few feet from the desk.

"Prince Aramis," the Prophet greeted. "I hope you are enjoying your stay here." Some of the priests snickered at the comment.

"What do you want?" Aramis asked tiredly.

"Is that any way to speak to your host?"

Aramis spat on the desk. One of the priests smacked him across the back of his head. His anger flared but the priests held him too tightly for him to do anything. He growled in frustration.

"Come now," the Prophet said, "do not act like an animal. We are civilized men here. Let us talk together as such." He walked slowly over to a small table and motioned Aramis to come near. When he didn't budge, the priests moved him by force.

Aramis recognized the map on the table. It was the same one he had seen previously when the Prophet had tricked him into retrieving the blood from the shrine. There were several red pins at random points.

"Those pins represent Mordum's agents," the Prophet remarked, as though reading his thoughts. "We have yet to discover the agent in Talvaard, but I am certain it won't be much longer. The elves of the Deadlands have launched an attack along the northern border of the kingdom."

The Prophet ran his finger along the map. "As the new king diverts his forces to the border, it will leave them vulnerable for attack. That is when I believe the agent will make his move."

Aramis wondered why the Prophet was telling him this. He couldn't care less about the agents of Mordum with the exception of one: his father's assassin. And he was likely the cause of Mel's death as well.

"Here in Oakvalor we know Mordum's agent is you. And since we have you as our guest, there's nothing you can do to further the cause."

The Prophet picked up a pin from a small wooden bowl at the edge of the table and pressed it into the map. This pin was green and was located in the Deadlands.

"My priests have found the whereabouts of the next item Mordum's followers are searching for. We don't know *what* it is, but we know where it is kept."

Aramis stared at the pin. He knew what was coming. The Prophet was going to ask him to retrieve it, perhaps because the only way in was to have the mark of Mordum. He smiled slightly, taking pleasure in the fact that the Prophet would not get his way this time.

"Have you ever been to the Deadlands?" he asked.

"What reason would I have to go there?" Aramis

answered.

"It was merely a question." The Prophet shrugged and continued speaking.

"The Deadlands is an unforgiving place. Its borders stretch from the length of Oakvalor past Talvaard. No one has mapped its end. Some speculate that the Deadlands have no end; that the desert stretches on for eternity." The Prophet chuckled to himself.

"Anyway, it is also the home of the elves. They are barbarians at best, marking their bodies with magical symbols and waging war against one another. My priests are still determining what has brought them forth to attack the human settlements. King Garrick certainly has a lot on his—"

"Can you spit it out already? I'm assuming there's something there you want? Something you think I'm going to *fetch* for you?"

The Prophet stared at him. "Straight to the point, I see. Very well. Located in the Deadlands far to the north is a place known as Red Mountain. At the top of that mountain is a building. Within lies what I seek. It is there you will go and find it."

Aramis shook his head. "No, I won't. I will not do anything for you. I did what you asked once and it brought nothing but the death of my friend. Then you imprisoned me. I refuse."

The Prophet was grinning. "You seem to be mistaken," he said. "I'm not asking you to go. My priests are taking you there. Your will in this matter is pointless."

Aramis felt his stomach churn. He considered the fact that it might be easier to escape while out in the open. That was a small light at the end of the tunnel, he supposed. He still didn't like the fact that the Prophet thought he would do whatever the man ordered.

Time to play along.

"How am I to get something if I don't even know what it is?" he asked.

"You will find out when you get there. The item is guarded by a powerful sorcerer. The sorcerer will know what the item is."

"And he is just going to give it to me?"

"Of course not," the Prophet answered. "You have to earn it. I only have so much of the details, but you have all of the information I have. My priests will take you to get cleaned up and you will leave first thing in the morning."

Aramis considered arguing further but decided against it. There was no use. Now he needed to figure out how he was going to escape.

"I have a request."

The Prophet's eyebrow rose in curiosity. "You aren't in any position to ask for anything." He paused. "But I will consider it."

"I only ask that you give me my dagger. Honor my request as a favor to Mel's memory."

The Prophet seemed taken aback. "The rusty piece of junk you were carrying? That's what you ask for?" The Prophet laughed.

"I would have figured you'd ask more than that, especially in honor of Melchiades's memory." He shook his head, still laughing.

"Very well. Make sure he gets the dagger before you set out tomorrow," he instructed one of the priests. "Now take him away from me."

As the priests led him out of the chamber, Aramis began forming his plans.

He has no idea what that blade can do, he thought to himself. It had pierced the scales of a phiebus. And soon, it would cut his bonds and he would be free.

"I am the only man worthy to be king."

—Adamar

CHAPTER 3

Adamar's footsteps echoed throughout the hallway as he walked toward the throne room. His freshly-polished boots clacked loudly against the stone floor, reminding him of a time long ago. A time when he had run through this very hallway as a boy. The walls were covered with beautiful tapestries and massive murals. His father certainly had good taste. Before Adamar had the templar kill him, anyway.

His two bodyguards followed behind him, flanked on either side. They were as silent as shadows. Other than the occasional ruffle of their robes, he would never have assumed they were there. As he approached the large doors that led to the throne room, the soldiers standing nearby hustled to open the doors for him. They saluted as he passed.

The chamber was crowded with the nobles. As soon as they noticed his presence, a hush fell over the room. He made his way to the throne at the back of the room and sat down, his two guards moving to the shadows behind the giant chair. Adamar tilted his head to either side until he felt his neck crack, then drummed his fingers on the armrest.

He had always admired the throne as a boy. It was elaborately decorated, with the backing of the chair carved to resemble a large Oaktree—the namesake of the kingdom. It was finally his. And all he had to do was kill for it. He smiled as he felt a great sense of achievement settle over him. He realized the nobles were all staring at him, waiting for him to speak. He motioned for the herald to come closer.

"Are the generals present?" Adamar asked.

The herald, a young boy of fifteen, nodded vigorously. "Yes, my lord."

"I'd like to hear from them first."

The boy bowed low and then turned to face the crowd. Cupping his mouth with his hands, he shouted, "The King requests the generals!"

Three men separated from the crowd of people and came forward, stopping at the bottom of the three stairs that raised the throne above the main floor. They bowed as well.

"What word?" Adamar asked.

The generals glanced at each other hesitantly before one of them spoke up.

"Nothing yet, King Adamar. The patrols are still searching, but they have yet to even find a trail. It's possible he has fled the country."

Adamar snorted in derision. "I highly doubt that. The traitorous coward is probably hiding. Have the patrols continue to search for him. I want him brought to me immediately when he is found."

"Of course," the general replied. One of the other generals cleared his throat. Adamar recognized him with a wave of his hand.

"King Adamar, some of the soldiers have gone missing."

"Missing? Were they killed?"

"I don't believe so," the general answered. "It seems they have abandoned their post."

Adamar leaned forward. "How many?"

The general swallowed nervously before speaking. "Twenty, including one of the Captains."

Adamar stood up. "I hereby declare deserters to be punished with death!" he thundered. "Anyone aiding a deserter will also be put to death. Is that clear?"

The crowd of nobles nodded or voiced their assent. Adamar sat back down and dismissed the generals. He waved the herald back over.

"You can run down the list in normal order now."

The next few hours were filled with boredom as he entertained the nobles' petitions. Petty land disputes, tax reports, the mundane things of running a kingdom that he didn't really care to do.

He'd have to find someone to do these things for him so that he could concentrate on more important matters. Such as finding his brother.

Aramis would be a pain in his side until he was found. Adamar hadn't decided if he wanted to kill him or lock him in the dungeon for the rest of his life. Although the templar had cursed Aramis with the mark, Adamar believed he would still prove to be problematic in the grand scheme of things.

Besides that, he now had reports that Ilias, Mordum's appointed Prophet, was demanding Aramis be kept alive because he was the chosen one to bring Mordum into the mortal plane.

Adamar scoffed at the notion. Obviously, Mordum would choose someone more suitable for the task. Someone like himself, or the templar. Someone strong and decisive, who took action without waiting around for specific directions.

After all, the blood from the shrine had been stolen from Ilias's temple, proving that the Prophet himself was inept. On top of having the soldiers looking for Aramis, he now had several patrols looking for the blood in case Aramis had left it with someone he trusted.

If he could track down the blood and retrieve the other two items needed, that would ensure his rise to Prophet. Yes, he would be second only to Mordum himself. The thought thrilled him.

Long after the nobles had left, he still sat on the throne musing about his rise in power. Servants eventually came and lit the candles, signaling night had come. Breaking his reverie, Adamar stood and left the chamber, his guards falling into step behind him.

"Is everything ready?" Adamar asked aloud.

"Yes," one of the men answered.

Adamar nodded in response. He walked through the twisting hallways and stopped at one of the many doors that ran the length of the wall. Pulling a small chain out from the neck of his shirt, he produced a small key.

Removing the chain from his neck, he slid the key into the opening on the door and turned it. A soft click sounded and he pushed the door open and entered the room.

It was faintly illuminated by a few candles. When one of his guards shut the door behind him, the candle flames flickered briefly. The shadows danced wildly in response, reminding him of the night he had committed himself to Mordum's service.

The room was sparsely furnished. A large chair, fashioned after the throne, sat at the back of the room. Directly behind the chair was a window that he'd had covered with a thick black cloth. He'd always been more comfortable in the dark. That had probably been one of the many warning signs to his parents.

On the ground a few feet from the chair was a large silver bowl. It gleamed occasionally in the candlelight. To the far left stood a rectangular table. Its only adornment was a wooden carafe and chalice.

Adamar walked to the table and looked inside the carafe. It was full to the brim with water. Partially unsheathing his sword, he ran his right palm along the sharp side of the blade. Pain lanced through his hand as it cut deeply into his flesh.

Lifting his hand over the carafe, he let the blood drip into the water. Awkwardly using his left hand, he re-sheathed the sword. He counted the drops of blood as they left his hand and hit the water. When the appropriate number had been reached, he pulled his hand away and pressed it against his leg.

He'd forgotten to bring something to bind it with and didn't feel like ripping his shirt. Pressing his palm hard against his leg for good measure, he removed his hand and grabbed the carafe. Careful not to let any of it spill, he brought it to the silver bowl.

Kneeling slowly, he poured the contents into the vessel. Once it was empty, he returned the carafe to the table, grabbed the chalice, and went to sit in the chair. Placing his hand over the chalice, he let the wound on his palm continue to drip.

His vision began to blur and he realized in the midst of everything, he'd forgotten to eat. The loss of blood was making him feel lightheaded and he feared for a moment he might pass out.

The dizziness was momentary and eventually passed. Placing the cup on the ground, he knelt down in front of the bowl and began whispering softly; chanting the words he had memorized like a fiery brand in his mind:

"Bind the light,
bind my soul,
use this knight,

to make you whole."

Adamar felt the air in the room immediately chill. A sound that reminded him of someone exhaling filled the air and the light of the candles was snuffed out. A presence, dark and sinister, filled the room around him.

"Rise, my servant."

Adamar stood up and looked into the corporeal face of his lord and master.

"Mordum," he managed to utter. The name filled him with power and his body shuddered. Suddenly lacking any control over his body, he fell backward into the chair. The room echoed with a screech as the chair's legs moved along the stone floor a few inches.

"Have you found my blood?"

It took a moment for Adamar to gain control of his body. The power of Mordum was intoxicating. It burst through every part of his body. He clenched his fists as he tried to keep the power within him, but it was no use. The power receded and he sat in the chair, weakened and frustrated.

"I am displeased to inform you that I have not found it yet," Adamar answered. "I have several patrols searching day and night for it."

Adamar could feel Mordum's anger as though it were something palpable. The feeling faded quickly.

"Very well. What of the other items? What of my bones and my ashes? Have your scribes found where they were hidden?"

"Not yet, but I am confident that they are getting close. As they scour through the history books, it becomes more and more evident that those who hid your body intentionally do not mention the locations.

"As we speak, they are looking through a book with a detailed account of your previous ... defeat." Adamar waited for a mental barrage of pain, but it never came and so he continued.

"This account is much more detailed than any others they have come across. It mentions the place they brought your body and what they did to it. To you. I am sure this account will name where they hid your bones and your ashes."

"What of your brother? Have you found him yet?"

"No."

"He evades even my eyes. I can feel him drawing closer to the Mark. It will not be long before his location is known to me. Continue searching. Do not summon me again until you have news that will please me."

"Yes, my master."

"There are glorious rewards for you if you succeed."

"I want the Mark," Adamar said, his tone almost begging.

"The Mark will come when I am ready to give it to you. Your faith continues to strengthen. Persist in the ways that I have called you and you will surely find pleasure. But if you fail me ... "

"I will not fail," he said adamantly. "I will do anything necessary to ensure your return."

"Good."

Adamar moved from the chair to the floor and grabbed the chalice. He held it up to Mordum and kept his eyes lowered. He felt Mordum take the cup.

"The only thing sweeter than the blood of my enemies is the blood of my servants."

The chalice clattered to the floor and Adamar felt Mordum's presence withdraw from the room. He grabbed the cup and stood up on shaky legs. His hand hadn't stopped bleeding and he was feeling weak again.

He managed to put the cup back on the table and stagger over to the door before he collapsed. The door opened and his two guards stepped in and picked him up, then carried him to his personal chambers.

They had servants bandage his hand and change his

clothes under their watchful eyes. They dismissed the servants and placed Adamar into his bed. One of them stood by the door and the other sat in a chair next to the bed.

As Adamar floated in and out of consciousness, he was vaguely aware of his bodyguards. Mordum's words became a litany in his mind, repeating them over and over.

But if you fail me ... but if you fail me ... but if you fail me ...

Though Mordum was God of the Dead, Adamar knew Mordum loved him. And he would give his soul to prove his devotion to his god.

—Jovanna

CHAPTER 4

The air ripped at him furiously, as if it were angry that he was flying through it. His clothes billowed about wildly and he found it hard to keep his mouth shut. The air hissed around him suddenly as he summoned his armor. It formed out of mist, slowly taking shape over his body. It was black as night with an upside-down red cross emblazoned on the breastplate.

Garrick hit the ground on one knee. The armor protected him, but he still felt the jarring force of the sudden stop. The ground beneath him shattered like pottery pieces. Dirt and stone debris filled the air.

After a moment the air cleared. He expected to be overrun by elves already. Then he realized there was complete silence. Elves stood staring at him dumbfounded. Beneath his helm, Garrick grinned wickedly.

He summoned his blade and the familiar hiss filled the air. It had been a while since he had summoned his armor and blade together. The feeling of power coursed through his veins.

Without warning, he charged into the elvish ranks, slashing and gutting anyone near him. After their initial shock wore off, the elves began to mount a defensive. They were too wary to get close enough to strike him, so he pushed into their defenses, forcing them to fight him.

Most of them carried crudely made swords and they shattered under the force of his blade. They came at him with spears and he easily sheared the tips off. His blade separated limbs, cut throats, spilled intestines and seemed as eager to drink his enemy's blood as a demon.

His armor was by no means invincible, and neither was his body. His arms began to grow heavy with exhaustion. He was drenched in sweat and blood covered his helm, making it hard to see.

Something heavy crashed into him from behind. He almost tripped and fell, but managed to get his feet steady. Then he turned and thrust his sword into the gut of the elf he assumed had struck him.

In the left corner of the slit of his helm, he could see more elves rushing toward him. He risked a glance behind him to see if his men had managed to seal the hole in the wall.

He could see several soldiers struggling to push back some of the attackers. He noticed that they were the odd skinned elves whose skin had deflected the arrows. He struck down another three elves and then rushed toward the breach.

He threw himself bodily into one of the elves and grunted in pain. It was like running into the castle wall. The elf turned to face him and Garrick swung his blade diagonally, using both arms to try and cut him from shoulder to hip.

His blade *clanged* in his hand and he almost lost his grip on it. Garrick was surprised to see that his sword hadn't even nicked the elf's skin. The elf smacked his own sword against Garrick's shoulder which didn't do any damage but sent him reeling backward. His armor and blade were blessed by Mordum himself. How could elven magic stand against Mordum's power?

As he considered the question, the elf came at him, slashing haphazardly. Garrick could tell he didn't have any formal training. His form lacked any discipline and he held his blade awkwardly.

Garrick lifted his own blade and slammed it against the elf's, snapping it in half. Then he launched a vicious kick at the elf's kneecap. It felt like he was kicking a boulder. Pain shot through his foot and he staggered back, trying to keep from putting pressure on it.

The elf grinned at him and began touching some of the tattoos on his arms. The symbols he touched began to glow with a faint bluish light. Garrick began to backtrack slowly but the elf closed the gap, striding toward him confidently.

Hands grabbed him from behind and he struggled to free himself. Within seconds he was surrounded by elves. They knocked his legs out from under him and forced him to the ground. He stared up at the approaching elf, his tattoos glowing brighter now.

Garrick's struggling was useless. The elves were holding him down. Sweat pooled around his eyes. He tried shaking his head to keep it from blinding him. The elf stretched his arm out toward him. Garrick gritted his teeth and tried to prepare himself for anything. Lightning flickered along the elf's fingertips.

Mordum help me!

Suddenly the elf's arm jerked to the side, the lightning from his fingers flying through the air into the group of elves holding Garrick down. He quickly snapped his visor up so he could see clearly and was greeted by a woman fighting with the elf.

He rolled onto his side and got to his feet. He snatched his blade from the ground and watched the woman. She gripped the elf by the shoulder and held her hand over his arm. He wasn't sure what she was hoping to accomplish, but then he noticed the hue of the elf's skin changing. It slowly turned from the grayish color to a light tan color, resembling more closely the other elves he had seen.

"Take his head!" the woman shouted at him.

"What?" he asked, confused. He was trying to figure out what she was doing and hadn't expected her to speak.

"Cut his head off!"

Garrick pushed the confusion to the back of his mind and with an easy swing of his sword removed the elf's head from his shoulders. The woman released her hold on the elf's body and it slumped to the ground. She was covered in blood but it didn't seem to affect her. She ran toward the breach and grabbed another one of the gray-skinned elves.

After a few moments, she commanded him to take his head. Garrick and the woman followed the same pattern for the remaining elves with the gray skin. When they had cleared the area, the men inside began sealing the hole in the wall. Garrick motioned to a large group of elves coming toward them.

"We've got company," he said.

The woman didn't bother looking. "Is there another way in?" she asked.

"On the other side of the castle. There's a hidden entrance in the wall. If we can get there without drawing attention to it, we can get in."

They sprinted off and ran along the wall, Garrick in the lead. While he knew there was a hidden door, he couldn't remember exactly where it was. The castle had one tower and he knew it was located on the same side, but it was intended to blend in and he wasn't entirely sure he'd spot it. His breath came in short gasps and he was drenched in sweat. He dismissed his blade so he could focus solely on running.

Garrick ran a few feet away from the wall and looked up, trying to locate the tower. They were roughly a hundred feet past it. He scanned the wall, looking for anything that might give an indication as to where the door was. He didn't see anything.

"Where's the door?" the woman demanded.

"It's here," he answered, still looking. "Somewhere."

"You don't know where your own secret entrance is?"

Garrick turned to her. He didn't like her tone.

"This isn't my castle," he said briskly. "This is my general's castle."

She grunted in response and walked to the wall, running her hands along the stones. Garrick looked back the way they had come and could hear the elves coming. They didn't have much time.

He ran over to the wall and started searching. He looked for loose stones, handholds, anything. And he found nothing. Just as he was about to give up and search further down the wall, he heard the woman give a triumphant shout. He jogged over to her.

"I've found it," she grunted as she pushed against the wall. "This stone has a mark on it."

Garrick looked closely and saw she was right. Etched lightly into the stone was a mark that looked like a keyhole. It wasn't deep enough to be an actual keyhole, but it looked just like one. He pressed his shoulder against the wall and helped the woman push. The wall didn't budge.

"The elves will be coming around the corner any minute," he said.

Suddenly the wall shifted inward and began sliding to

the right. Garrick stepped back and watched as the section of wall disappeared into the rest of the wall. There stood Rycroft and several armed men.

"My lord," Rycroft said, the relief evident in his voice.

"General," Garrick greeted. "The elves are closing in."

Garrick let the woman go first, then he followed. The soldiers pushed the section of wall back into place. On either side of the section were two "U" shaped steel bars sticking out. The soldiers dropped a large wooden plank into them.

"The door opens from the inside?" Garrick asked.

Rycroft nodded. "It's intended to be an escape route." The general led them out of the tunnel and into the courtyard. Garrick dismissed his armor and it disappeared in a swirl of mist. Everyone stared at him but he ignored their unvoiced questions. He ran his hands through his sweat filled hair.

"Is the breach sealed?"

"Uh … yes, sir. That section of the wall is obviously weakened, but it will hold for now. The engineers have given us the news that they are low on the supplies needed to fix it properly."

"We need to keep the elves away from the wall," Garrick said.

"What do you propose?"

That was a good question.

"Arrows have proven ineffective. Hitting the gray-skinned ones is like hitting a stone wall. I nearly dropped my sword when I struck one of them."

He looked at his hand and flexed it. It was a little sore, but otherwise undamaged.

"Stone skin," the woman said. Garrick and Rycroft turned to her. He had almost forgotten she was there.

"Excuse me?" Rycroft said.

"Stone skin," the woman said again. "That's what it's called. Their ability to deflect your arrows with their skin. It's a tattoo some of them have. It makes their skin like stone."

"How do we get around it?" Rycroft asked.

"You don't," she answered.

"*You* did it," Garrick pointed out. "You did something that changed their skin color. What did you do?"

"That's none of your business," the woman replied.

Garrick frowned. *I really don't like this woman.*

"I helped you get inside to safety. The least you can do is tell me how we can defeat them."

"Fair enough," she answered. "Are you a wizard?"

Garrick shook his head. "No."

"Are you?" she asked, turning to Rycroft.

"No," he answered.

"Then there is nothing you can do. Even if you were wizards, there is a very specific ability I have that few other wizards possess. It allows me to see magic."

"I have seen magic before," Garrick said.

"That's not what I mean," the woman answered. "I mean actually see magic. The …" she seemed to struggle for the right word, "specks of … magic that makes up a spell."

Garrick thought she looked flustered. "How does that help you?"

The woman sighed. "I can see how the tattoo works and I can control the magic flowing to it. I can't destroy the tattoo, but I can weaken its power enough to inflict bodily harm."

"She could help us," Rycroft said.

"She's only one person," Garrick pointed out. "There are thousands of warriors outside these walls. Who knows how many of them have this stone skin? There's no way to gather that information."

"Who says I would help you anyway?" the woman said disdainfully.

"You are bound by the laws of our kingdom to help the king in any way you can," Rycroft retorted.

"He's not *my* king, he's yours."

Rycroft eyed her closely. "You aren't from Talvaard?"

She snorted. "Of course not. When is the last time your kingdom has seen a wizard?"

Rycroft remained silent for a moment. "She's from Oakvalor," he said, glancing to Garrick.

"I assumed as much," he said. "And as such, she's a welcome guest. If you don't want to help us, I understand. My authority has no sway over you. But I can assure you that if the elves manage to push through further into Talvaard, they will do the same in Oakvalor. The people of your kingdom will suffer the same tragedies."

The woman rolled her eyes. "You're assuming I care."

Garrick tilted his head curiously. "Who are you? What's your name?"

"Jovanna," the woman answered. "My name is Jovanna."

—Melchiades

CHAPTER 5

The next morning, Aramis and ten priests left the temple and headed north toward the Deadlands. The temple of Edria was in the city of Kaldore, which was a two-day journey northeast from Oakhaven, the capital of the kingdom. While Aramis had never been to the Deadlands, he knew the boundaries and landscape of his country.

To get there, they'd have to travel through the countryside where the majority of the people were simple farmers, then through the Tylhem Forest. Aramis remembered hearing stories from some of his teachers about the forest.

Some said it was haunted, and others that a mystic race of beings called it home. It had interested him as a child, but as he considered it now he found it to be foolish.

The priests rarely stopped to rest. When they did, it was to relieve themselves and eat something quick.

Aramis had attempted to escape a couple of times using the power of the mark to run with quickened speed as he did when running back to the temple.

Unfortunately, it didn't work. At first, he suspected it meant the mark wasn't working, but he later determined it was the shackles they had put on his wrists. Something about them seemed to negate the power of Mordum's mark.

He began to study each of the priests, watching their mannerisms and how they held themselves. Although they didn't seem to have official titles, he quickly discovered who the leader was. It was obvious by the man's demeanor. He issued orders subtly and dictated their pace and their breaks. The others appeared to be lowly apprentices, perhaps just the "muscle" for this trip.

Other than pushing him when he started lagging, the priests ignored him for the most part. He didn't bother trying to talk to them, instead spending his time thinking about how to get away and where he would go if he managed to succeed.

Perhaps he would head to Talvaard and ask Garrick to assist him. He remembered that the Prophet mentioned Talvaard being under attack by the elves. If that were true, Garrick had his own problems to worry about.

Aramis sighed in frustration. He felt so lost and helpless without Mel. His friend had been a wise advisor, someone he could trust and rely on. Now … he bit his lower lip forlornly.

The farther north they traveled, the warmer the air got. He knew that once they entered the forest the heat would be much worse. As they passed through a small village, some of the priests broke away from the group to resupply their provisions.

The rest of the group continued to the outer edge of the town and waited for the others to return. After roughly twenty minutes the others met back up with them. One of them pulled the leader to the side and conversed quietly with him. Aramis attempted to get closer without being noticed. He only heard bits and pieces of the conversation.

"That's what the farmer claimed," one of the priests said.

"When did they pass through here?" the leader asked.

"Yesterday. They didn't interrogate anyone, but they made it clear who they were looking for. Seems they shook the townsfolk up a little. They don't see soldiers often."

The leader nodded. "They're looking for him …" he trailed off as he noticed Aramis looking at them. "Find us somewhere to stay for the night, preferably somewhere out of sight."

The priest nodded and left to do as he was commanded. Then the leader came over to him.

"It seems the soldiers of the king are out here looking for you," he said to Aramis.

"To arrest me for a crime I didn't commit, I'm sure," Aramis replied.

"Fortunately for you, the Prophet still has need of you. They won't find you. At least not for now." He walked off before Aramis could reply.

Aramis considered how this new information would impact his escape attempt. It was possible he could elude both the priests and the soldiers if he got away, especially this far out.

A little while later, the group headed to a barn to spend the night. The town was so small and visitors so few that the town didn't even have a proper tavern or an inn. They would all have to sleep on the floor of the barn. Despite the fact that there was a thin layer of hay on the ground, Aramis still found it uncomfortable. The priests took turns keeping watch.

He lay there staring at the rafters of the barn, unable to sleep. It seemed like hours passed before his eyes started to get heavy. As he closed them and began to drift off in the darkness, a sound outside startled him. He sat up and looked around. The priest keeping watch must have heard it as well, for he seemed on edge and kept looking out into the night. Aramis heard it again. He thought it sounded like a gentle thump against the side of the barn.

The priest at the door hesitated for just a moment before he stepped out of the barn and into the blackness of the night. Aramis looked at the other priests. They all appeared to be sleeping. Just as his muscles tensed and he decided to get up and make a run for it, the priest appeared in the doorway. Aramis slumped back against the ground.

Blast it, he thought. The priest took up a new position at the door and stared out into the night.

Heaving a sigh, Aramis tried to get back to sleep. It took him a while because of his sudden excitement at the possibility of escape. Eventually, he finally drifted off back into sleep's embrace.

● ∞ ● ∞ ●

Aramis woke to one of the priests nudging him with his boot. He grunted and slapped the man's foot away. Rolling onto his side, he realized everyone was awake and moving except him. He got up and stretched before brushing strands of hay off his clothes. Aramis noticed the priest was still standing there.

"You done, Your Highness?" the priest said sarcastically as he performed a mocking bow. When he realized Aramis wasn't going to say anything in retort, the man handed him a small bread roll and an apple.

"Here's your breakfast. If you get thirsty, there's a

horse trough outside."

Aramis took the food and left the barn. It was after sunrise already. The sun had probably been up for almost an hour, possibly two, if his guess was correct. He ate his breakfast fairly quickly, not realizing how hungry he was. Then he walked over to the horse trough.

It was a long wooden box filled with water. Aramis dipped his hands in, flinching at the coldness. He wasn't expecting that. He noticed small bits of foam floating in the water. It was probably horse saliva.

With a shrug, he held his breath and dipped his head into the box. He came up sputtering and coughing. The cold had caused him to inhale sharply, and he sucked in some water.

Laughter broke out behind him and he turned to see some of the priests looking in his direction. He gritted his teeth in anger and tried his best to ignore them. He let the water drip dry from his hair and face.

As the priests were collecting their meager belongings and getting ready to head out, Aramis noticed one of them was standing off to the side, looking out into the woods. He watched the man curiously, wondering what he might be looking at. He made a subtle motion with his hand, so subtle that Aramis almost wondered if he saw it at all. Then he turned and joined the other priests. He was keeping his head down.

Aramis found the actions odd but gave it no further thought. He didn't care if the priests were crazy, as long as they didn't bother him any more than they already were. He walked over to where they were gathered.

He must have missed a conversation between them because as he reached the group, they began to walk north without orders from the leader. Two of them took up positions beside him. One of them was the man who had acted oddly.

He looked at the priest and noticed the man was

staring at him. When they made eye contact, the priest winked at him. Aramis scrunched his face in confusion and looked away. The man had probably spent too long as a priest.

When was the last time any of these men had seen a naked woman?

They continued their trek north, leaving the small town behind and nothing but farmland as far as they could see. They walked for several hours before stopping for a short break. Aramis slumped down onto the ground and pulled his boots off and began furiously rubbing his feet. His feet were sweating profusely and his skin was beginning to rub on the soles of his boots painfully.

He watched the leader of the group and knew that he'd force them to continue walking. He surveyed the landscape as he continued rubbing his feet. A few hundred feet ahead was a small copse of trees. Aramis heard the leader and one of the priests talking.

"Is that Tylhem?" the priest asked.

The leader shook his head. "No, but I think we are close. Maybe a mile past those trees there—if this map is correct."

"Why would the map be incorrect?"

The leader pulled a rolled parchment from his robes and unfurled it.

"Because it's fairly dated."

Aramis saw him point to something on the map. Then he rolled it back up and stuff it back into his robes.

"What of the rumors?"

The leader scowled. "I don't believe in folklore."

"Every rumor has a seed of truth to it," the other priest countered.

"Be that as it may," the leader replied, "that will not stop us from entering the woods. Let's get moving. The faster we can get to our destination, the faster we can get back to the temple."

Aramis put his boots back on and stood up. His feet were sore, but there was nothing to be done. The tattoo on his arm didn't seem to help with soreness, only open wounds. The other priests got up and started walking again. The two who were guarding him took up their positions again. Aramis began limping along as best as he could.

As they continued their trek, the pain turned from a dull soreness to excruciating before finally numbing his feet completely. His steps became sluggish. He ground his teeth in annoyance. One of his guards shoved him from behind.

"Keep up," he growled.

Aramis managed to keep from falling. He turned and shot a murderous look at the priest. He guessed it must have caught the man off-guard because he hesitated. Someone touched his arm and he snapped his gaze to them.

It was his other guard. He smiled disarmingly and nodded with his head to keep moving. Something about the man's attitude calmed Aramis's anger and he reluctantly continued.

They walked for about ten minutes. Aramis's pace was steadily slowing, but the priest who pushed him didn't say anything. They were nearly to the grove of trees when the leader motioned for them to stop.

"We're going to camp here for the remainder of the day until morning. At sunrise, we'll—"

His words were cut off as an arrow ripped through the back of his shoulder, spinning him in a violent circle. Chaos broke out among the priests as more arrows rained down among them, striking the ground around them as well as the priests. Cries of pain and fear filled the air.

The guard who had smiled at him removed his robes

and threw them to the ground, then grabbed Aramis's arm and pulled him toward the trees. Aramis struggled against the man's grip and tried to escape.

"Stop fighting, my Lord!" he yelled. "Follow me!"

His words confused Aramis. Only his loyal subjects called him Lord. Pushing his reservations aside, he stopped fighting and followed as fast as he could. They broke through the tree line and when he saw who was firing the arrows, realization suddenly dawned on him. They stopped running after they got a decent distance into the woods.

Aramis slumped to the ground, pressing his back against the trunk of a tree. He could feel his heart racing and he tried to catch his breath. He looked around the wooded area and saw several men in armor, all of them wearing his family's crest and colors. These men were soldiers of the crown. He felt greatly relieved until he remembered what he'd overheard the day before.

These men have been looking for me.

He felt worms of fear squirming in his stomach.

"They're going to take me back to the castle in chains," he breathed to himself.

He had to run while they were occupied with the priests. He rose to his feet and turned to head further into the woods when he noticed the man he had followed was standing there, his blade drawn.

"It's good to see you," the man said with a smile.

"Is it?" Aramis asked, his tone revealing his suspicion.

"Yes, sir. We've been looking all over the countryside for you. The Captain wanted to find you before anyone else. Ah, here he comes now."

In a quick movement, he cut the shackles that bound Aramis's hands. Aramis assumed they must have been old, for they broke easily under the man's blade.

He turned to an unexpected but familiar face.

Kaldrick approached with a wide grin.

"My King!" he greeted loudly before embracing Aramis in a tight hug.

"What in Hell's name are you doing way out here?" Aramis asked in surprise, returning the man's embrace.

Kaldrick was impressively strong and his hug crushed the breath from his lungs. The captain released him when he started coughing. Aramis backed up a step and appraised the Captain.

It had been a few months since he had seen the man. He didn't look much different. He was as tall as Aramis, though much more muscular. His upper arms were as thick as some of the branches that littered the ground around them.

His hair was black and cut short, almost to the point of being shaved. He was wearing a hauberk without the sleeves, supplemented by bronze lamellar. The lamellar consisted of small platelets that were punched and laced together in horizontal rows, adding more protection to the torso. Aramis liked the look of it.

"We're out here looking for you! Been searching a few weeks now. You have no idea how glad we all are to have found you. The man who has usurped your throne has patrols out at all times trying to hunt you down. I was praying I would find you first."

"He'll get suspicious when you don't check in," Aramis warned.

Kaldrick laughed heartily. "I'm sure he's more than suspicious now," he replied. "We deserted our post. I'm sure there's a bounty on ours heads same as yours."

Aramis shook his head. "You need to go back. I don't want anything to happen to you men because of my situation."

Kaldrick waved his hands in the air. "I won't hear it, my Lord. We are loyal to the end, regardless of how that end may turn out. If we die, we will die fighting for a cause we believe in. No one left unwillingly, I assure you of that."

Aramis knew there was no sense in arguing with him. The man was as stubborn as they come, which added to his battle prowess. He had sparred with the captain a few times and Kaldrick never once bowed out, no matter how exhausted or injured he was. Truth be told, Aramis was glad to have him.

"Very well, Captain. How many men do you have with you?"

"There are twenty of us," Kaldrick answered.

Aramis nodded, considering again what he had thought about many times since leaving the temple. One of the soldiers approached, handing a water skin to Kaldrick. The captain took a long drink and handed it to Aramis. He drank a couple of mouthfuls and poured some onto his head. The chilled water ran through his hair and down his face and neck, cooling him off.

"What was the plan assuming you found me?" Aramis asked.

Kaldrick shrugged and rubbed the back of his neck, slightly embarrassed. "I didn't think that far ahead to be honest. Nevertheless, we are at your disposal. What did you have in mind?"

Aramis took another drink from the skin and handed it back to the soldier who brought it.

"Are the priests dead?" he asked.

Kaldrick looked to the soldier for the answer. The soldier put the stopper in the water skin and shook his head.

"No, sir. The majority of them have fled, but there are a few wounded that they left behind."

"Thank you …" Aramis paused expectantly.

"Jonn, my Lord."

"Thank you, Jonn."

The soldier bowed and left. Kaldrick stared at Aramis

intently. "I see your wheels turning, sir."

"One of the wounded should have a map on him. I need it."

"I'll retrieve it myself," Kaldrick said.

"I'll come with you. I have a message for him to take to his prophet."

They left the woods and walked to where three bodies lay in the grass. The soldiers had gathered around them awaiting orders. They all bowed as Aramis approached. He looked to each of the bodies.

One of them lay very still and Aramis wondered if the priest was dead. He tried not to think about it and knelt beside the priest with the map. The arrow that punctured his shoulder was at an odd angle. It looked quite painful. His robes had a pool of blood near his thigh.

Aramis lifted the cloth up to take a look. It wasn't as bad as it seemed. The skin had a clean cut that was probably from an arrow that had grazed him.

"You'll live," Aramis informed the priest. "When you get back to your temple, I want you to deliver a message to your prophet. Tell him I'm not a fool. I know what god really holds his allegiance, and it isn't Edria. It's Mordum."

The priest's face scrunched up, but Aramis didn't know if it was from the pain or his words.

"If you don't believe me, consider why he wants the items that will bring about Mordum's entrance into this world. Also consider why he isn't bothered by the death of Mel, one of Edria's most faithful." Aramis paused at this, fighting back his emotions. He clenched his jaw and spoke through gritted teeth.

"Tell him I will retrieve the next item, but he will *never* see it!"

Aramis snatched the map from the priest's robes and stood up. He looked around at all of the soldiers and finally settled his gaze on Kaldrick. The captain raised his eyebrows in expectancy.

"Leave the priests here. If they die, so be it."

"Yes, my Lord."

Aramis walked back towards the woods and Kaldrick fell into step beside him. They walked in silence for a few moments before Kaldrick spoke.

"Why didn't you order them killed?"

Aramis considered the question.

Why indeed? he wondered.

There were numerous reasons at the tip of his tongue, but he settled with the one that made the most sense to him amidst his whirling emotions.

"They are not the reason I am out here as a captive. They are following the orders of someone above them, someone who holds a position of power. They are culpable for their actions, obviously, but I cannot blame them for following orders. Killing them would not make me any better of a king, nor would it satisfy my anger and hurt."

Kaldrick remained silent, but his demeanor told Aramis that he approved of his reasoning. He hadn't noticed it before, but the air in the woods was humid, overwhelmingly so. He began sweating almost immediately. Aramis let Kaldrick take the lead.

As they made their way further into the woods, Aramis noticed a small camp was set up. Tents were strung up between the trunks of large trees. In the center of the camp was an enormous tree stump that had been converted into a makeshift table.

When they reached the stump, Aramis unrolled the map and laid it on the surface. He used a few small stones to hold the parchment down and examined the map. The priest was right: the map *was* outdated. The numbers in the lower left corners of the map marked the year it had been drawn. It was almost a hundred years old.

Kaldrick held out a biscuit. "Hungry?"

Aramis accepted it and ate without tasting it. He stared intently at the map, considering his next course. Finally, he pointed to a square symbol on the map.

"Have you ever been to the Deadlands?" he asked.

"I have not," Kaldrick answered. "There's nothing out there worth seeing. At least that's what everyone says."

"I need to go there. Here, specifically. It's some sort of castle or fortress. This map indicates that it is at the top of Red Mountain. Ever heard of it?" He looked at the captain.

Kaldrick shook his head. "No. Why do you need to go there?"

"It's a long story," Aramis sighed. "I don't expect you and your men to come with me, but if you do I will tell you everything on the way."

"I've always wanted to travel," Kaldrick said with a grin.

"I appreciate your loyalty," Aramis replied. "I have to warn you that this journey will be perilous."

"All journeys are in their own way," the captain said.

Aramis turned his attention back to the map. He eyed the path the priest had chosen. It seemed the best course, so he decided they would continue following the route.

"This forest here," he pointed, "have you ever heard of it?"

When the captain didn't answer, he looked up. Kaldrick had a troubled look on his face.

"What is it?" Aramis asked.

"Well, it's ..." Kaldrick looked down at the map. "I can't read."

As he considered it, Aramis wasn't surprised. Most soldiers were only trained for battle, not academics. Only those from wealthy families typically paid for both.

Aramis shrugged.

"No matter. It's called Tylhem Forest. I overheard some of the priests talking about it. They seemed overly superstitious about the place."

"I've heard stories," Kaldrick said. "Most of them as a child. It's rumored that the place is filled with druids, though nothing has ever been confirmed."

"What's a druid?" Aramis asked.

"Old men of magic. They usually keep to themselves. Supposedly they prefer the company of animals to other men. Harmless unless provoked." Kaldrick shrugged. "That's all I know. And most of it is hearsay."

"Our path takes us through it," Aramis said, waiting to gauge the captain's reaction.

Kaldrick merely nodded.

"Will the men have an issue with it?"

"Some of them may be a little wary, but they'll be fine."

"Good. We leave in the morning before it gets too warm."

● ∞ ● ∞ ●

Aramis walked toward the woods, his men following behind him. It was silent. A disturbing silence, devoid of the normal sounds of the night. Not even the creatures that came awake in the dark were making noise.

Aramis was walking across an open field. The tall grass swayed gently from a breeze he couldn't feel. Not far ahead he could see the tall, dark silhouette of trees rising up from the landscape. As he drew close to them, he could hear a voice drifting on the wind.

"Do not enter."

A robed figure stepped out from the tree line. He held his hand up before him, warding the way. Aramis stopped and looked back. His men were no longer there.

He wondered where they went and how they left so suddenly. The robed figure pointed back the way Aramis had just come from.

"Do not enter these woods."

"We only want to pass through," Aramis replied, confused.

The trees swayed suddenly under a strong wind. The figure stepped back into the trees, disappearing from Aramis's view.

"You have been warned."

Aramis's eyes snapped open. He was burning up and covered in sweat. He got up and pulled his shirt off, then left his tent and walked to the outer edge of the camp where he noticed a fire was burning. He sat down on a large rock next to the fire and stared into the flames, considering his dream.

It was different than the others. The figure had warned him not to enter the woods, but it wasn't the oppressive dreams he normally experienced since having the mark of Mordum. He looked up when he heard someone approaching. It was Kaldrick.

"Can't sleep?" he asked quietly.

Aramis shook his head. "I had a disturbing ... dream."

"That makes two of us," Kaldrick said.

Aramis's heart quickened in his chest. "What? What did you dream about?"

"Barmaids that weren't loose women," Kaldrick said with a snort, shaking his head.

"I've never even heard the like before. Must be all the time we've spent outside of civilization." He sat down on the ground beside Aramis and stretched his legs toward the fire.

Aramis felt a huge sense of relief. He feared that Kaldrick might have experienced the same vision-like dream he had. He looked at the mark on his arm. The black cross stood out in stark contrast against the color of his skin.

"Are you a religious man?" Aramis asked.

"Not really," Kaldrick answered. "I know there are forces or powers or whatever out there that we don't understand, but that doesn't mean I follow them. What about you, my Lord?"

Aramis opened his mouth to answer the question, then hesitated. He really wasn't sure that he was religious, but he had seen things that could not be explained.

"I've always said I didn't believe in divine beings," he said, "but recent events have caused me to re-evaluate that belief. I know there are gods, but like you, I have not chosen to follow any of them."

Aramis traced his index finger along the dark shape of the mark and felt the pull of its power. It was tempting to fall into the power it offered, but he knew it was nothing more than a façade. Mordum offered nothing but death and destruction. If there was such a dark force as Mordum, then certainly there must be a power on the side of good.

He considered Mel's goddess Edria. The Prophet was evil, but did that mean that Edria was evil as well? Or was it possible that the Prophet had simply turned away from her path?

Given how Mel had modeled his life, Aramis highly doubted that Edria was evil. He leaned back on the rock and looked up into the sky. The foliage of the trees blotted out most of the heavens, but he could see a few stars twinkling against the black sky. He heaved a long sigh and stood up.

"I'm going to try and get back to sleep," Aramis said. "We've got a long road ahead of us."

Kaldrick nodded. "I'm not far behind you."

Aramis returned to his tent and eventually fell asleep.

● ∞ ● ∞ ●

Aramis woke to the sound of voices and the clattering of metal. Apparently, the entire camp was awake already. He rolled out of bed and put his shirt on, then grabbed his boots from the corner of the tent and slipped his feet into them. The balls of his feet were still sore from walking the day before, but he knew they had to get moving. There was no time for weakness. Not now.

He stepped out of his tent and was surprised to find Kaldrick and his men had packed up almost the entire camp. Aramis looked at his own tent and decided to take it down. He knelt down and just as his hand touched the rope that was staked into the ground, he felt a hand on his shoulder. He looked up to see Kaldrick smiling and shaking his head.

"Don't worry about the tent," he said. "The men will tackle that. You need to get some food before we pack up the cooking supplies." Kaldrick motioned toward the front of the camp, close to where the fire had been the night before.

"You'll get no argument from me," Aramis answered. He stood up and went to see what was left. He was greeted with smoked sausages and a leg from a turkey. The soldier in charge of cooking informed him that they had been lucky and found a group of the feathered birds that morning.

Aramis thanked him and ate as he watched the soldiers break down his tent. He downed the sausages pretty quickly and bit into the turkey leg. It had an odd taste to it. It wasn't a bad flavor, but it wasn't all that great either.

"Beggars can't be choosers," he muttered to himself and took another bite. The men moved quickly and efficiently to break down the tent. Before he had finished eating they had it completely packed up and ready for their march.

Aramis stripped the leg of the majority of the meat and then tossed the bone into the brush. He licked his fingers before wiping them on his pants, then went and relieved himself. After washing his hands and face in a small pool of water he had come across, he met up with Kaldrick and unrolled the map he had taken from the priest.

"We're still agreed on the path through Tylhem?" Aramis asked.

Kaldrick nodded. "Yes, my Lord. Some of the men are a bit skittish, but not enough to bail out."

"Good to hear. Well then, let's get moving."

Aramis was surprised at the organization of the men under Kaldrick's command. With little guidance from him, they collected their belongings and began marching out of the woods. They headed north toward Tylhem Forest, moving at a decently quick pace.

Scenes of his eerie dream kept running through his head. He tried to ignore them, tried to think of something—*anything*—other than the mysterious man who had given him an ominous warning, but it was useless.

They traveled for a while, walking across flat grasslands. There was a gentle breeze blowing which helped to make the heat of the day tolerable. In the distance, not more than a quarter mile, Aramis could make out an expanse of trees. Judging by the distance they had traveled, he felt certain it was Tylhem. That and the fact that the forest seemed to stretch across the horizon.

The map he carried had given a large amount of space to mark the forest, but Aramis had assumed that whoever had drawn the map was being generous. Now that they were closing in on it, Aramis didn't think the mapmaker was even close.

Kaldrick called for a break, and they all stopped a few feet from the boundary of the forest to drink water and rest their legs. After a few minutes of rest, Kaldrick called two men over and gave them instructions to scout out the front of the forest. They trotted off into woods, disappearing among the thick underbrush.

"They are decent at scouting," Kaldrick said as he approached.

"I trust your judgment," Aramis replied. He lowered himself to the ground and then lay on his back, blotting the sun out with his hands. "How long before they come back?"

"Ten, maybe fifteen minutes. I told them to do a quick run through of the area, nothing too detailed. We haven't seen any signs of life this far north, so it's unlikely we'll run into anything other than wild animals."

"Sounds good," Aramis yawned. His eyes were getting heavy. Now that he thought about it, he felt fairly exhausted from the march. "I'm just going to lay here a minute. Rest my eyes a little."

Kaldrick nodded.

Loud screams split the air and Aramis quickly sat upright, his heart pounding in his chest. The men were running towards the woods. Aramis scrambled to his feet, trying to figure out what was happening.

"Where's everyone going?" he shouted to no one in particular.

"Women!" one of the soldiers yelled. "There are women in there!"

Aramis scanned the tree line but didn't see anything. He looked for Kaldrick but didn't see him. The man must have already entered the woods. As he started toward the forest, a powerful wind picked up, making the tall grass weave violently. It whipped his clothes about wildly and his shirt made a flapping noise. Thunder rumbled in the distance. Aramis picked up his pace as he saw the last soldier disappear in the brush.

He entered and tree line and pushed into the thick brush. It was noticeably darker in the forest. The wind rustled the foliage overhead. He could see the branches swaying from the force of the wind. And then he heard the shouts.

They were faint at first, but as he continued deeper into the woods, they became louder. Aramis lowered his head as he walked, trying to keep the thin branches of saplings out of his face. Finally, he broke through the brush and was surprised to find a path. It was well worn and had signs of recent footprints.

Kneeling down, he studied the prints and recognized the familiar shape of boots. The men had come this way. As he followed the trail that wound through the woods, the shouts he heard earlier were gone.

It was silent, with only the occasional sound of the wind moving through the treetops to let him know he hadn't gone deaf. He followed the path deep into the forest. It wasn't just a long walk. It was hot and humid, making his shirt stick to him.

A while later, he entered a small clearing. Small shacks were spread out among the trees, but he didn't see anyone. Upon further investigation, he realized the buildings weren't shacks at all.

They were made up of tree roots, extending from the ground to make small home-like structures. He glanced into a few of them. The contents were fairly basic: beds, tables, and chairs—all made of tree roots and vines.

The path he followed into the clearing picked back up on the far side the small residential area. Aramis continued following the trail, still not hearing much other than the wind. Tree branches creaked ominously and the leaves seemed to whisper at him. An eerie feeling began to worm its way into his gut.

The path wound between trees and under low hanging branches. Insects bit at his exposed arms, raising small itchy bumps along his flesh. He thought he could see things moving among the shadows. He walked for a lot longer than he cared to, wondering just how far into the woods the path went. Just as he was about to turn back, the path dumped him into another clearing, this one smaller than the first.

The glade was one of the oddest things he had ever seen. It was almost a perfect circle, ringed by large, thick trees. The ground was flat and dark brown, devoid of any grass or leaves.

And then he saw the body. There, lying in the middle of the clearing in a puddle of blood, was Kaldrick. Aramis ran to his still form and knelt down beside him. He was breathing. Aramis sighed in relief. That was a good sign. Kaldrick was covered in blood, but it didn't seem to be his own. Kaldrick's eyes fluttered momentarily before finally opening.

"What happened?" Aramis asked softly.

"There were women," he answered weakly. "Naked as newborn babes. We chased after them, but I don't have any idea why. Something I can't explain came over me. It came over us all. And then … and then …" he shuddered and shook his head.

"Easy now," Aramis said. He looked around the clearing, but there were no signs of the other soldiers.

"We have to leave," Kaldrick whispered urgently.

"Why? Where are the others?"

Kaldrick lifted a shaky hand and pointed to one of the trees that ringed the glade.

Aramis stared in confusion. "What is it? I don't—"

And then he saw it. The tree had a face. Aramis rose and got closer. It was definitely a face. There was also something oddly familiar to it. It kind of looked like …

Aramis backed away from the tree quickly when he saw the face move. It was one of the soldiers. He could see the vines and bark of the tree had covered the man almost entirely. One of the man's hands was uncovered and his fingers twitched spasmodically.

The tree was eating him. A feeling of dread came over him when he heard a familiar voice behind him. He turned around slowly to find the man from his dream standing over Kaldrick.

"I warned you not to come here."

—Prince Aramis

CHAPTER 6

Eighteen Years Ago

"Do it quickly and quietly."

The written words echoed in Osen's mind as he watched the young man that was celebrating at the bar. The tavern was somewhat dead for the night compared to the normal flow of people that visited the run down establishment. Considering what he had been tasked with, he considered that a blessing. Fewer witnesses.

Osen felt the heavy bag of gold at his waist. It was enough to secure his future for the rest of his days. He could buy an estate somewhere quiet and never work again. And all he had to do was kill someone. He had killed before, of course. Usually in back alley brawls, and once when he robbed someone. That one had been an accident.

His attention shifted from the drunken revelers to the barmaid serving them. His eyes widened in surprise when he saw that she was pregnant. She wasn't too far along judging by her size, but her stomach stuck out enough that it was noticeable. He swallowed hard. No one had told him the person—the *woman*—he'd be murdering was pregnant. He felt a flush of anger at the lack of information.

Snatching his mug off the table, he drank the rest of the ale. He wiped his mouth with his forearm and rose from the table. He tossed a few of the gold coins onto the table after a long look at the pregnant barmaid. Shaking his head, he left the tavern and walked around to the stables where he'd left his horse.

"I'm a killer, but I'm not killin' no baby," he muttered to himself. He considered tossing the gold into a ditch but decided not to. No one would know if he didn't go through with the job seeing as how he'd never actually met his employer. They had exchanged letters in random locations and Osen was always careful to ensure no one saw him.

He retrieved his horse from the stable boy and led the mare out of the stable. He was about to mount up when he felt the call of nature. Slipping the reins around a wooden pole next to one of the watering troughs, he walked into the shadows at the edge of the tavern and relieved himself. When he turned around, he was startled to find two men standing there.

"If I hadn't just gone, you boys would have scared the piss outta me," he said with a nervous laugh.

"You aren't thinking of leaving, are you Osen?"

Osen took a step back and tried to make out their faces in the dark. "Jace?"

"Not quite," the other figure spoke. "Did you kill the barmaid?"

"N-not yet," Osen stuttered. "I was just checkin' on mah horse."

"Good. I'd hate to think you were going to run off with my money without completing the job you *willingly* accepted."

"Now hold on. No one said anything about killin' a baby."

"You weren't asked to kill a baby. You were asked to kill a woman."

"Yeah, but she's preg—"

"I'm well aware of what she is," the man snapped irritably. "Get in there and kill her."

"In the middle o' the tavern?" Osen asked dumbly.

"If you have to," the man answered. "Or bring her out here. Either way, just get it done."

Osen nodded and stepped around the man. He wasn't completely sure, but he thought he saw the glint of metal as he passed the larger of the two men. Gooseflesh covered him as he considered what he was about to do. Leaving his horse tied to the pole, he made his way back around to the front of the tavern. For a brief moment, he considered running off into the night. It was the cowardly part of him, he knew. For some reason though, he had a feeling he wasn't going to be alive much longer.

He stepped back into the building and went back to the table he had been sitting at. His empty mug and the coins he'd left were gone. He sat down and began thinking of how he was going to get out of his situation. He didn't want to kill an unborn baby. He took no issue with killing a woman, but a baby? Absolutely not. He knew then why they had offered so much money for the job. How many others had turned it down?

"I'm sorry, I thought you had left."

Osen jumped at the words and looked up to see the barmaid. "What?"

"I thought you had left, so I cleaned up the table. Want me to bring you another drink?"

"No thanks," Osen managed to say. "I won't be here much longer."

"Ok." The woman smiled and left to another table.

After seeing her up close, Osen realized she was younger than he thought. She couldn't have yet reached twenty years. If he had doubts before, they had doubled now. She was younger than his daughter. Granted he'd not seen her since she was born, but he'd kept track of her age as the years passed. How would he feel if someone snuffed her life out?

He slammed his fist onto the table. The room went quiet and he realized everyone was looking at him. Some of the looks he got were curious while others were of concern. He ignored them and began tapping his fingers on the table. He didn't see any other way out.

"Screw it," he muttered to himself. Standing back up, he walked over to the barmaid as she was cleaning off a table.

"I need to talk to you," he said, trying not to speak too loudly.

"Sure," she said as she looked up from her work.

"Not here. Somewhere … private."

"Ah," she said with a knowing grin. "I would, but I'm spoken for. I don't think he'd appreciate me double-dealing on him."

"What? No, not that." He glanced around the room and lowered his voice. "There are two men outside who are here to kill you."

If his words scared her, she didn't show it. She continued wiping off the table, then gathered up a couple of empty mugs and made her way toward the bar. Osen followed her. The woman set the mugs on the end of the bar where an older man retrieved them and disappeared into the kitchen.

"I think you're drunk and need to sleep it off," she said.

Osen shook his head. "I'm not drunk. They …" his mouth suddenly went dry. Why was he going to tell her anything? What was it to him if someone killed her? He didn't know her and it was none of his concern. But he knew it was wrong.

"They hired me to kill you," he blurted out. He quickly looked around to see if anyone had heard him. The revelers made it hard to hear anything and no one appeared any wiser.

"I took the job because o' the money." He grabbed the bag from his waist and opened it, showing her the contents. "I came here ta kill yah, but I din't know ye was with child. I tried tah leave, but they met me out back. They mean tah see yah dead."

Perhaps it was the tone of his voice, but she looked like she believed him. Her face had gone pale and her hands were shaking.

"I'm going to help yah get out," he said. "I won't be killin' no baby, and I won't be lettin' someone else do it neither."

She nodded and removed her apron, tossing it carelessly onto the counter. She went into the kitchen and came back a moment later carrying a travel sack. Osen led her out of the tavern, pausing as they stepped outside to let his eyes adjust to the darkness. He put his finger to his lips and walked quietly toward the road that wound through the small town. The woman followed him, but she kept her distance. They followed the road for about twenty minutes before breaking the silence.

"Is there somewhere safe ye can go?" he asked.

"I can go home," she answered.

"I dun't think that's a good idea. They may know where ye live. What about ye'r man? Does he live nearby?"

When she didn't answer, he looked over his shoulder to see if she was still following him.

"There is no man," she said. "This baby is the result of a bad decision."

Osen didn't know what to say so he changed the

subject. "Where are we going?" he asked.

"My house isn't much farther. Just beyond the trees there."

He had no idea what he was going to do after he got her to her house. He didn't want to stick around, but he also wasn't excited about leaving her alone. It didn't appear that anyone had followed them. As the woman had said, her house wasn't far. It was small and shabby. Not that he was judging. His bed was usually the floor of a bar. She took the lead as they got closer.

When they reached her doorstep, she lit a lantern that hung on a hook next to the door. Using the flame of the lantern, she lit a candle and entered her house. Osen turned and surveyed the darkness around the house. He didn't hear or see anything out of the ordinary, so he followed her into the house.

The candle lay on the floor, sputtering. His heart began to pound and he drew his dagger. Looking into the shadows, he saw the woman lying face down on the ground. Had the men followed them after all? He warily reached down and picked up the candle. Shining it into the shadows, he didn't see anyone. Kneeling beside the woman, he shook her.

"Hey … are ye ok?" he whispered.

She groaned. Relief flooded him. He'd feared she was dead. She rolled over slowly.

"Adamar?" she asked.

"Adamar?" Osen repeated confusedly. Then he realized she was looking past him. Dread filled him as he rose to his feet and turned around. The two men from the tavern stood in the light of the candle.

"Good evening, Tasia," one of the men said. "It's been a while."

Osen held his dagger out threateningly and stood over her.

"Don't hurt her," he said.

"I don't want to," the man responded, "but unfortunately, I don't have any choice in the matter. You see, the child she carries is mine. And I can't have illegitimate kids running around when I become king."

"King?"

"Yes. Now if you don't mind, please kill her."

Osen looked from the prince to the woman. Her face was contorted in a fearful expression. The prince wanted him to kill someone? From what he'd heard of the king, that didn't seem like something he'd condone. He struggled internally, unable to decide what he should do. Something hard struck the back of his head and his legs stopped holding him up. He fell onto the floor and watched in horror as the bigger man in armor drove his sword through the woman's stomach.

She screamed in agony. Osen burst into tears and began sobbing uncontrollably. The prince pointed at him and said something he didn't hear. The other man jerked his sword out of the woman and came at him. The last thing he saw was the prince smiling in delight.

—Prince Aramis

CHAPTER 7

Garrick wrapped a chunk of bread in a cloth and stuck it into his pack. He'd already packed cheese and a few apples as well. Slinging the pack over his shoulder, he left the pantry and made his way through the castle hallways. None of his men had volunteered to go to the Deadlands, so he'd decided to go himself.

It was a risk in many ways, but he could not think of any other option. None of the generals had really voiced much opposition. This concerned him mainly because he had worked hard to reunify the kingdom and feared that the men would tear it apart in his absence. With the threat of elven invasion, however, they might stay focused. All he could do was hope.

He entered the courtyard and was greeted by all of his generals. They regarded him in silence and he wondered what they all might be thinking. Nothing ill-intentioned, he hoped.

"I will send word back as soon as I find their women

and children," Garrick said. "I expect to find this place still standing and not overrun by elves. Whatever it takes, you must work together to keep our people safe."

A few of the men nodded their agreement. Garrick looked to each of them in turn, his gaze lingering longer on those whom he didn't fully trust.

"My King," Rycroft spoke. "Please take an escort with you."

Garrick shook his head. "No. The more people traveling together, the more likely we are to be seen. We need to enter the Deadlands with no suspicion from the elves. I will take one soldier to send back word with me as we discussed."

He thought Rycroft would argue further, but he didn't. "Where is Kelvin?"

"Here I am, my Lord."

Kelvin was handpicked by Garrick. The man was strong and well versed in battle. And he was devoutly loyal. Garrick knew if he got into a rough situation, Kelvin would be a great ally. He also knew he could trust Kelvin to get word back to them once they found the elven camp in the Deadlands.

"Let's get moving then," he said. The generals followed Garrick and Kelvin to the concealed passageway that led out of the castle. He slid the door open and stepped out. He glanced around to make sure there were no elves present, then he turned to the men. "Wait until you see my signal to create the diversion."

Kelvin stepped out of the doorway and the generals closed the door again. Now that Garrick knew where it was, it was a little easier to see the outline of the door amidst the wall. He jogged around the castle toward the eastern side where he hoped to use the coverage of some woods to hide their journey. A few miles of walking and they'd be out of Talvaard and enter into the Deadlands. He'd never been there before, but he knew it would be radically different than the grasslands that surrounded him now.

It was still early and the sun had yet to rise. Garrick paused at the edge of the castle wall and peered into the gloom. He could make out the shapes of tents and see their campfires, but he did not see any movement. He waited a moment longer, then sprinted across the landscape toward the trees. Kelvin followed close behind him, the sound of their steps dulled by the tall grass.

While they ran, Garrick turned around and jogged backward. He made a whistling noise that resembled the sound of a bird. A few seconds later, the sound was returned. He turned back around and continued running.

They reached the grove of trees without alerting the elves. Garrick paused for a few minutes to catch his breath, then headed north. He took care of where he stepped, not wanting to snap twigs or make loud noises. The faster they could make it to the desert without interruption the better, but he also knew that stealth was important. At least until they were far enough away. By now his men should have been raining flaming arrows down among the elven camp.

It took them several hours, but they eventually reached the edge of Talvaard's borders. The tall grassy plains slowly started to transform. Here and there large patches of sand splotched the landscape until finally, they could see the desert stretch out before them. There was nothing but sand as far as Garrick could see. Large hills that stretched for miles across the horizon cropped up from the flatter ground. They stopped to eat a light lunch. They had passed a stream earlier and had filled their canteens with fresh water.

"Drink light to conserve your water," Garrick instructed Kelvin. "Who knows when we might see water again out there."

"Yes, sir."

"Are you ready for this journey?" Garrick asked.

"I am, sir."

Garrick turned his gaze over his shoulder and took a long look at Talvaard. He thought about praying to Mordum and asking to keep his people safe but thought better of it.

Why would the God of the Dead protect the living?

They set off at an easy pace, but it didn't take long before Garrick was drenched in sweat. The sun was in the middle of the sky and there wasn't a cloud to be seen. The desert air was dry and suffocating. His throat became parched and his mouth felt like it was made of cotton. He continuously spat foamy saliva out and drank sparingly of his water.

He began to wonder if he had made the right decision. From all he had read, the Deadlands was aptly named. There were slithering creatures that could kill a man with a single bite. Getting overheated in the dry air could cause hallucinations. There was the possibility of dying from thirst.

All of these facts floated around in his mind, mingling with the thoughts of his people. He thought about his wife back in the capital of Talvaarin. She was safe there for the time being. If the elves pushed further into Talvaard, there wouldn't be anywhere safe for anyone. His steps became slower the longer they traveled. It became a monotony in the back of his mind:

Left leg. Right leg. Left leg. Right leg.

He looked back to check on Kelvin and could see he was struggling just as much as himself. Their eyes met and Kelvin nodded. Garrick returned the nod and they kept walking. That was another reason he chose Kelvin for this task—he was stubborn. He would push himself to his breaking point before giving up. Garrick admired that trait in men. Not so much the stubbornness, but the ability for a man to be able to control his body with his mind.

Garrick was having trouble keeping track of how much time passed. Other than the position of the sun in the sky, there was nothing to indicate they were even moving. They trudged uphill and down. Several times they had to stop and dump the sand from their boots. The grains rubbed against the bottom of his feet, scouring the skin off. He wasn't bleeding, but it was a bothersome pain.

They stopped and set up camp as the sky began to darken. Garrick was surprised at how quickly the temperature dropped as the sun descended. Kelvin began setting up their tent. He'd offered to carry it along with his pack for which Garrick was thankful. He'd had enough trouble carrying his own pack and trying not to collapse from the heat. There was no wood to make a fire, so they ate a meager dinner and retired into the tent.

As Garrick lay down, he knew his face had been burned from the sun. His skin was sore and hot to the touch. He felt extremely dirty as his sweat dried.

"This is going to be a long walk," Garrick whispered to himself.

"Yes, it is," Kelvin answered.

Garrick chuckled softly. They hadn't talked much at all the entire day. He was tired and wanted to get to sleep, but felt obligated to talk with his traveling companion.

"How are you holding up?" he asked.

"I've seen worse days," Kelvin answered.

"Me too," Garrick said. "Are you married?"

"No, sir."

"Is there a woman you fancy?"

A moment of silence. "Yes, sir."

"You can stop calling me sir."

"Yes, sir ... er, O ... okay."

"Does she know?"

"Know what?"

"Does she know that you fancy her," Garrick clarified.

"I don't know," Kelvin answered. "I've had a few gifts delivered, but I never let her know who was responsible for them. I'm trying to work up my nerve."

"That's the mystery."

"What's that, sir? I mean … Garrick."

Garrick smiled in the darkness. "That men like us can go into battle with nerves of steel, fight off our enemies, take a life if necessary. Yet when it comes to approaching a woman, we sputter and make fools of ourselves."

"I thought I was the only one," Kelvin admitted.

"Nonsense. You should have seen me when I began courting my wife. I was like a frightened dog running from its shadow."

They both laughed at that.

"You should tell her you like her," Garrick added. "Once this is all over."

"I think I will," Kelvin said.

"I think I'm going to sleep now."

"Me too."

Reminiscing of the early days with his wife, he fell asleep with a smile on his face.

● ∞ ● ∞ ●

Garrick awoke to the world spinning around him. He grunted as something heavy slammed into him. He realized it was Kelvin. The tent wrapped around them and Garrick could hear the sound of the tent flapping wildly. They tumbled over each other several times before coming to a jarring halt.

Managing to escape the tent through a tear in the fabric, Garrick crawled out to a nightmare. The wind was blowing so hard that sand had filled the sky and blotted out the sun. The stinging sand quickly blinded him and he covered his face with his hands. He heard Kelvin start cursing and figured the man was in the same predicament.

His eyes were watering which made matters worse. The sand was now encrusted around his eyes. Dropping to his knees, he placed his head between his legs and resigned himself to wait until the storm passed.

Eventually, the wind died down enough that he was able to start cleaning the sand from his face. His eyes, ears, and even his nose were caked with it. Using the last of his water and the hem of his shirt, he was able to remove the majority of it. Finally able to see again, he found Kelvin had wrapped himself in the tent. He helped the man untangle himself from it.

Working together they attempted to break down the tent. In the process, they found it had been ripped in several places.

"It's almost unusable," Kelvin remarked.

"I agree," Garrick replied, kneeling down and studying a long tear in the material. It was almost a foot long.

"We don't have anything to patch it with, but maybe we can salvage some of it."

Garrick generally tried not to let things get to him, but he was starting to feel the weight of their task. He stood up and eyed the position of the sun.

"I'd say it's mid-morning," he guessed. "I'm out of water and we now have no shelter from the elements. We're only a day's march into this blasted place and already we're at a disadvantage. Not to mention we have no idea what direction we should be searching in."

Kelvin remained silent.

"This place is bigger than I imagined it to be." Garrick heaved a sigh and stared at their surroundings, trying to decide what to do.

"Sir," Kelvin said.

"I told you yesterday you don't have to call me that."

"Sir," Kelvin repeated, his tone more urgent. "Don't move."

"What?" Garrick froze mid-turn. "What is it?"

And then he heard it. An odd rattling noise and a hissing sound.

"It's a snake," Kelvin answered, speaking softer. "And it's right beside you."

Garrick shifted his head slowly and looked down. The snake was coiled up, its tail flicking back and forth faster than his eyes could keep up with. It was less than two feet away from his left leg. He feared if he tried to move away, it would strike him. Eyeing the distance, he suddenly had an idea. He lifted his hand a little. The snake tensed and for a moment Garrick thought it was about to come flying at him. Fortunately, it didn't move.

He didn't realize he was holding his breath until he felt the pressure building in his lungs. He forced himself to breathe normally, then he summoned his blade. The air hissed as it formed. He blinked and almost missed seeing the blade fully form, slicing the snake's head off. Its body began floundering about. He leaped away and dismissed his blade.

"That was close," he said. He looked to Kelvin and saw the man staring at him.

"What was *that*?"

Garrick smiled disarmingly and shrugged. "I've been blessed."

"Blessed?" Kelvin asked.

"You could say that."

"Blessed with a black blade of Mordum? Where is your mark?"

Garrick's heart began pounding. "What?"

Kelvin's gaze hardened. "So it's *you*. You are

Mordum's agent in Talvaard. How … how could you betray your own people?"

"You are mistaken," Garrick answered, holding his hands up.

Kelvin shook his head. "You seemed so honorable, so respectable. I should have seen through your act."

"I am not whatever it is you think I am," Garrick said. "I've never followed the tenets of Mordum."

"Yet you summon one of his blades? The evidence against you is not good."

Garrick watched as the air around Kelvin began to shimmer with mist. Gleaming silver armor shaped around him and a long silver blade formed in his hands. On the right side of the breastplate, Garrick recognized the symbol of Zevea: a sun with outstretched wings. The Goddess of Light.

"Prepare to meet your dark god," Kelvin said. He lifted his blade and approached threateningly.

"Blast it," Garrick muttered as he summoned his own armor and blade. He brought his blade up and took a defensive stance.

"I don't want to fight you," he said.

"Then you will die quickly," Kelvin replied.

Garrick braced himself as Kelvin charged him. The blades clashed together with a loud *clang*. Garrick didn't want to fight his own soldier. He stayed on the defensive, parrying Kelvin's thrusts and back-stepping. He could tell by Kelvin's body language that he was starting to get angry. Garrick knocked Kelvin's blade aside and threw himself to the ground, rolling away to put some distance between them.

He got back on his feet and brought his sword up. Just as Kelvin began to rush at him, a loud cry startled both of them.

"STOP!"

They both turned to see an unexpected sight. An

elderly woman pushing a wooden cart. Wrapped around her eyes was an old dirty bandage. Garrick stared in confusion, even more so when Kelvin dropped to his knees and lowered his head.

"Who are you?" he asked.

The old woman smiled.

"Every man shapes his own destiny."

—Garrick

CHAPTER 8

Aramis stood motionless. The man from his dream was *real*. The man didn't move, but he was standing uncomfortably close to Kaldrick. He wore loose fitting brown robes that had a hood pulled over his head. He didn't seem very tall.

"What have you done to my men?" Aramis asked, slowly walking toward the druid.

"I haven't done anything to them, Prince Aramis."

"How do you know my name?" Aramis ceased walking.

"I know much more than your name, but that is not important. I warned you not to come here, and yet you still entered these woods."

"It was a dream," Aramis replied. "*You* were a dream."

"Yet here I stand."

"What's going on? What happened to my men?"

"Come with me and I will explain everything."

Aramis eyed the druid warily. He certainly didn't trust the man. He pointed to Kaldrick. "Step away from him."

The druid did as he asked and backed away from him. Aramis strode forward and helped Kaldrick to his feet.

"Don't trust him," Kaldrick said.

"I don't," Aramis answered.

"I'm not asking you to trust me," the druid said. "I'm asking you to follow me and to listen."

Aramis debated whether or not he should. If he refused, would the druid cast some spell on him? Perhaps turn him into a tree as well? He didn't know anything about druids, whether they were good or evil. He glanced back at the tree that seemed to be eating one of his men not thirty feet away. He made his decision.

"Lead the way," Aramis said.

The druid turned and led them along the path through the woods. He led them deep into the forest. Aramis gradually noticed a difference in the air. It was cooler and the sounds of birds and other animals filled the air. He hadn't realized it before, but he hadn't heard any sounds earlier. There was something about this part of the woods that seemed more … lively.

The path took them to a small wooden bridge that crossed over a gently flowing river. The druid led them across the bridge and the sound of voices filled the air. They entered a glade similar to the one Aramis had found earlier, with small huts made of vines and tree roots spread out along the clearing. Aramis saw men, women, and even a few children present. They were all busy, some cooking at small fires outside their huts, others carrying firewood, and still, others carrying baskets of fruit and vegetables.

"What is this?" Aramis asked curiously.

"This is our home," the druid answered.

"I saw another clearing like this one, but it was empty."

"Yes."

The druid didn't elaborate, and he didn't press the man. The people of the village took notice of Aramis and Kaldrick, but they didn't stare or point like other places Aramis had been. The druid led them to a long table that was being set up for a meal.

"Leave your friend here," the druid said.

Aramis frowned. "I will not leave him alone."

"He will be taken care of, I assure you. You can rejoin him shortly."

Aramis didn't want to leave Kaldrick, but he didn't sense any danger from these people. He looked around the village. The people were going about their normal duties and not paying them any attention. He leaned in close to Kaldrick and lowered his voice.

"I don't like the idea of leaving you here alone, but I don't think these people will do anything. Can you stay here while I talk with the druid?"

"They are different than the others," Kaldrick replied. "I'll be fine."

"The others?"

"The ones that …" Kaldrick shuddered and refused to say anything else. He sat down at the table.

"Help yourself to the food," the druid said, his tone comforting. "The meal will be ready soon." He motioned for Aramis to follow him and they walked to one of the huts. This one was slightly larger than the others. Aramis hesitated for a moment before following the druid into the hut.

The inside of the place was nothing like what he expected. The floor was made of smooth marble. The walls were covered with tapestries and paintings that had exquisite detail and the ceiling was painted with a beautiful mural of the night sky. There were hundreds of stars and they almost seemed to glow as though they were not merely painted on.

"How—"

"It is an illusion," the druid answered before Aramis could finish speaking. "It reminds me of what I left behind for the life I have now."

"You weren't born a druid?"

The man laughed. "Not many are born into this life," he answered. "Most of us got tired of the cities, the crowds of people, the hectic pace of life passing too quickly. No, most of us have chosen this life after forsaking the places we once called home."

Aramis was stunned. *Why would anyone want to leave civilization for this?*

The druid retrieved two wooden cups from a cabinet and poured some sort of colored liquid into them. He handed one to Aramis. When he didn't drink it, the druid smiled.

"It's just wine."

Aramis waved the cup under his nose and sniffed. It smelled sweet. He took a sip and was pleasantly surprised by the taste. It made his tongue light up with pleasure.

"It's good," he said. "Very good."

The druid set his cup down and pulled the hood back from his head. Aramis guessed the man to be in his fifties, possibly late forties. He was mostly bald, with only a thin ring of white hair that rounded his head above the ears. His eyes were a striking dark blue. His skin was a light tan color.

"So what happened to my men?" Aramis asked. He still wanted to know what was going on.

The druid picked up his cup and took a drink. "Before I can explain that, I must tell you some other things first. I've been living here as a druid for over twenty years. The ring of trees where you found your friend, that is a sacred place for us. It's been a sacred place for as far back as any of the druids can remember. We believe that Edria, the Goddess of Light, once walked in that very place."

Aramis finished off the wine in his cup. He was familiar with Edria and nodded. The druid refilled his cup.

"We go there to pray each day. Recently the area has taken on a different feeling. Dark whispers drifting on the wind that bespeak wicked sayings. Things in the shadows scurrying just outside of your view. Unnatural things." The druid made a sign in the air.

"I'm sorry, but I don't have time for a history lesson," Aramis said. "I've got something important that I need to do. The longer I'm held up; the more danger everyone faces."

"I know well the danger that presents itself," the druid replied. "For it is dwelling here in our forest."

"What do you mean?"

"You are familiar with Mordum?" The druid pointed to the tattoo on Aramis's arm.

Aramis rubbed at his arm. "I'm not a follower if that's what you are asking."

"You'll get no judgment from me," the druid replied. "Who a man chooses to serve is his own business. I merely asked because I noticed his mark on you and thought you might know what has happened to our forest. Our sacred place has been infected by Mordum. Something is happening in the realm of the gods, though what exactly no man knows. Unfortunately, we mortals are caught in the middle."

"What do you mean Mordum has infected the forest?"

"Do you remember the trees you saw earlier?"

"How could I forget?" Aramis said. "It was eating one of my soldiers."

The druid nodded. "That is part of the blight Mordum has caused. The forest itself turns against us. The village you first encountered that was empty … we had to flee that area. We've had to come here to this clearing. And yet the darkness of Mordum spreads further into the woods every day. Before long, we will have to flee this area as well." The druid finished his wine and set the cup on the table.

Aramis digested the man's words. While these woods were on the very edge of his kingdom, it was still part of his realm. What could he do for these people? How could he possibly help them against a god? *What would Mel do?* He downed the rest of his wine and set the cup down. The druid went to refill it, but Aramis shook his head.

"I need to keep my head clear," he said. "Have you tried using your magic against this blight?"

"Yes, though it hasn't done much. Mordum is God of the Dead. There is no force stronger than death, I fear. We managed to push the blight back at first. At least it appeared that we had. But it spread much more quickly than I thought possible. The darkness corrodes our spells, disintegrating them into oblivion."

"Do you know where it started?" Aramis asked.

The druid nodded. "I have a good idea," he said. "It's not far from the sacred ring of trees. There is a black patch of grass. One of the children noticed it after things started changing. We tried healing spells on the grass, but we might as well have been throwing dirt on it for all it accomplished."

Aramis massaged his hands over his face and rubbed his eyes. He was exhausted. He looked at the druid, considering his next words.

"If there were a way to stop the blight, what do you think it would be?"

The druid scoffed. "If I knew that, we'd have already

stopped it."

"I'm sorry," Aramis said, waving his hands in the air to mollify him. "Let me rephrase it. What is the opposite of death?"

"Life," the druid said without hesitation.

"Exactly. If Mordum can use the power of death to bring destruction to the forest, there must be a way to reverse it. Or at the very least, combat it."

"With what? Our magic is no good against his power."

"With the power of life."

The druid frowned. "If you are talking about human sacrifice, you are out of your mind."

"That's not at all what I'm talking about," Aramis replied. "I'm talking about using the power of life, not taking someone's life. There has to be some sort of spell that creates life."

"It's not a spell," the druid said. "That's called being a god."

"I'm not talking about *creating a life*. I'm talking about harnessing the power of life. Is there nothing like that you are aware of?"

The druid was silent for long moments. "Nothing that I can think of. I'll consult with the others and see if they know of anything. But even if there is a spell that powerful, how would it work? The one who casts it has enough trouble keeping the spell going. Where would they harness enough energy to combat death and power the spell?"

"Can spells feed off of people?"

"Yes, but that's dangerous. Take too much, and the person will die. It is forbidden among the druids to use another's energy."

"There are always exceptions to rules," Aramis replied.

The druid shook his head. "I don't like it. I will not

risk the life of one of my people to try something we don't even know is possible."

"You won't have to."

"What are you talking about?"

"I will let them use my life force."

The druid stood speechless. He moved his mouth as if to answer or offer up some sort of argument, but no words came out.

"I know the risk," Aramis said. "And regardless of it, your people are citizens of my kingdom. I will do what I must to aid you. If it doesn't work to save your home, at least I tried. I cannot leave you in a time of need as if it doesn't bother me."

The druid finally collected himself. "You have your father's heart."

"I appreciate that," Aramis said. "Have you heard the news of my father?"

"We don't get many visitors," the druid replied with a smile.

"Of course," Aramis said, feeling stupid for having asked. "He was murdered."

"No!" The druid was aghast.

"It is true," Aramis said. "I was there. An agent of Mordum killed him. I tried to stop him, but I was no match for him. I found out later it was one of Mordum's knights."

"A *templar*," the druid said in awe. "I have heard of these men if men are what they are. I am surprised you are alive to share this tale."

"He cursed me with this mark," Aramis said, pointing to the tattoo. "It is always difficult trying to explain that I am not one of his followers because of this thing."

"Why?" the druid asked.

"Apparently his followers receive the mark when they choose to follow him, and it is a lifelong commitment."

"I see."

Aramis sighed heavily. "I need to get some rest."

"Of course," the druid said. "You can rest here in my home. Dinner will be ready soon. I'll confer with the elders and see what I can find. Do you need anything?"

"No, thank you."

The druid left the hut. Aramis looked around the place. The illusion of the place was so realistic. There was a single chair that formed out of the wall. It appeared to be formed of a tree root and shaped to look like a chair that laid back. Aramis sat down on it and laid back. It was surprisingly more comfortable than he thought it would be. He closed his eyes and thought about what lay before him.

His life had been so simple a few short months ago. He'd never imagined life would take him where he was now. An exile in his own kingdom. His father murdered. His best friend dead. He was suddenly aware of how alone he was. Everything had been so crazy the last few days, he hadn't had time to think. Now his thoughts assailed him. The same images kept running through his head. His father dying before his eyes. Mel standing in the road prepared to give his life for him. His thoughts turned to Lord Bavol, one of the nobles in the court.

Aramis wondered how he was faring in his attempt to gather support for Aramis to take his throne back from the man who had usurped it. The old blind woman had said the man was his brother. Aramis still had his doubts about that. The truth would be known soon. And if the man was his brother, Aramis would never accept him. There had to be a good reason why his parents would have never told him about having a brother. According to Bavol, the men who served him had the mark of Mordum. Was the usurper a follower of Mordum as well?

Aramis could feel the welcoming darkness of sleep

coming over him. He fought it at first. It wasn't a good idea to let his guard down among people he didn't know. Eventually, he stopped fighting and gave in. His dreams were twisted and dark. He saw his home engulfed in flames, his people massacred in the streets. And then he was in the forest standing in the sacred tree ring, watching his soldiers being consumed by the trees.

He walked out of the ring and saw a patch of black grass. As he approached it, the ground around the grass began to move erratically, as though it were liquid. He knelt down and placed his finger on the ground. His entire arm disappeared into the ground. He quickly pulled it out. His arm was clean. No dirt; nothing. His mind couldn't understand what was happening. He stood up and placed his foot in the same spot. His leg up to his knee disappeared into the ground. He pulled it out and noticed the thing as he did with his arm.

It was clean. No dirt, no grass. He stared at the black grass in confusion. An arm grabbed him on the shoulder and started shaking him. He cried out in surprise and tried to pull away. The shaking grew more insistent. Aramis tried to push the arm off. He couldn't see who it belonged to. When he tried to look, the person's face was just a shadow. The arm started pulling him forward, dragging him toward the grass.

Aramis's eyes snapped open. Kaldrick stood over him, a hand on his shoulder, shaking him. "My Lord?" he said questioningly. "Are you okay?"

Aramis looked around and realized it had all been a dream. He sighed in relief. "I'm fine," he answered. "I was having a nightmare. There was this black grass that …" he trailed off.

"What is it?" Kaldrick asked.

Aramis quickly got up from the chair. "I think I know how where to find the cause of the blight."

"The what?"

Aramis realized Kaldrick had no idea what he meant. "Where is the druid who brought us here?"

"I haven't seen him. Why?"

"I need to find him. Come on." Aramis left the hut, walking at a brisk pace. He looked around the clearing but didn't see the man. A woman walked by carrying a small basket.

"Lady," Aramis called out. "Where is the man who lives here?" He motioned to the hut behind him.

"I think he's talking with the elders."

"Where can I find them?"

The woman nodded toward the path that led into the woods. "I saw them go that way. They may have gone to the sacred tree ring."

Aramis sprinted to the trail. He hoped he wasn't too late.

● ∞ ● ∞ ●

Aramis and Kaldrick arrived at the ring of trees and found the druid elders conversing quietly. Aramis was out of breath and had to calm his breathing before he could speak. His calve muscles were burning fiercely and his throat was dry. He looked over at Kaldrick. Other than the fact that he was sweating profusely, he would never have known Kaldrick just ran through a humid forest. Aramis approached the druids and was about to call out to the man he'd talked with earlier, only to realize that he still didn't know the man's name. The group of men turned to greet him.

"Prince Aramis," the man he'd spoken to earlier addressed him. "I have bad news. None of us know of any spells like what you described."

"I had a dream … or a vision. I'm not sure which. But it does not bode well. Show me the patch of black grass."

"It's over here," the druid led him outside the ring of trees to a grassy area. Most of the grass was a vibrant green. Fallen leaves and twigs littered the area. In the center of the grass was a circular dark spot that stood out in stark contrast. If Aramis didn't know any different, he would have thought it was nothing but ashes. He stepped forward but the druid blocked him with his arm.

"This place gives off a foul aura," the druid said. "It may not be safe to get any closer."

"I have to see something," Aramis replied. He pushed gently past the druid's outstretched arm and knelt down right outside the dark splotch. He held his breath as he reached down and poked the ground with his finger.

Nothing happened.

He pulled his hand back. It was clean. He exhaled in relief. Yet he was also frustrated. Where did the blight originate? He'd thought for certain his dream had been some sort of sign. He stood up and turned back to the druid.

"I thought I would find something here," he said, shaking his head. "I don't understand."

"What did you hope to find?"

"In my dream, this was a portal of some kind. When stepping on the ground, it sucked my leg into it." He turned back and stared at the grass. A feeling of dread slowly came over him. The hairs on his arms stood on end. He began backing away.

"What is it?" the druid asked.

"I don't know," Aramis answered. "I have a bad feeling about this place." The tattoo on his arm began to tingle. He tried to ignore it.

And then the black grass erupted into the air. Aramis cried out in surprise and jumped back quickly. A large creature climbed up out of the ground. Its skin was a shiny gray color, reminding Aramis of metal. It was manlike, with two legs and two arms. It had no hair on its head. Its eyes were like snow with bloodshot lines snaking through the white. Its teeth were jagged and looked razor sharp. The druids began chanting in a strange language.

The creature moved much quicker than Aramis expected. It ran at one of the druids and swiped at him with its clawed hand, cutting a deep gash into the man's neck. Blood spurt from the wound uncontrollably. The druid clutched at his throat as he fell to the ground, writhing in agony. The chanting of the other druids quickened.

Aramis was about to turn and flee into the woods when he saw Kaldrick charge the creature and tackle it to the ground. He suddenly felt foolish. If he ran, he was nothing more than a coward. He said he wanted to help these people, and at the first sign of danger, his first instinct was to run. That should not be the character of a leader. Especially not a king. Aramis drew the small dagger he had used to kill a phiebus with and charged into the fray. Kaldrick and the creature rolled back and forth, pummeling each other with blows.

He waited until they rolled around and the creature was on top, and then he plunged the dagger into the creature's back. It jerked away and growled in pain, causing Aramis to lose his grip on the hilt. The creature knocked Kaldrick in the head once more, got up, and turned to face Aramis. Suddenly the chanting came to an abrupt stop. In a move of stupidity, Aramis turned to see why they had stopped. And then the creature was on him, knocking him to the ground and scratching his arms and chest with its claws.

The scratches immediately began to burn and itch. He struggled against the creature, trying to get back to his feet. Suddenly he was free. Aramis scrambled to get up. He looked around frantically, trying to see where the creature was. And then he saw it—fighting with another creature. The new creature looked like a tree in appearance. It was covered in bark and had small, thin branches coming off of its body with tiny green leaves sprouting along the branches. Though it resembled a tree, it had legs and arms that looked humanoid. Aramis watched in fascination as the two creatures battled viciously. Kaldrick startled him when he limped up beside him. Aramis jumped and then laughed nervously.

"You scared me," he said, shaking his head.

"I didn't intend to. Are you all right?" he asked with concern.

Aramis looked down and noticed his arms were slick with blood. He hadn't even noticed. Using his hand, he wiped the blood off his left arm. The cuts were already healed.

"I'm fine," he answered. "What about you?"

"I'm a little banged up."

They sat in silence as the two creatures continued to fight. The tree looking creature appeared to be winning. It grabbed Mordum's gray creature by the throat and lifted it into the air. It kicked at the tree creature's chest, cracking some of the bark.

Aramis tore his gaze away and looked for the druids. He saw them gathered around their fallen comrade. He walked over to them quietly. The man he had been speaking with since arriving into the woods had tears in his eyes, but he remained fairly composed.

"I'm sorry," Aramis said, looking down at the dead druid.

"Jared was still young," the druid lamented.

Aramis didn't know what to say to that, so he didn't say anything. He wasn't much for religion, but he offered up a silent prayer for the man to whoever might be listening. Aramis's attention was drawn back to creatures.

"What are those things?"

"I don't know about the creature that came out of the ground," the druid replied. "The other one is an elemental. They are powerful creature wrought of magic and nature. In the past, we have used them for manual labor, but according to history they have been used in times of war."

"I thought druids were peaceful?" Aramis asked.

"We are. There are times, however, when peace does not solve problems. There are times that call for war, though we find them to be rare."

The elemental slammed Mordum's creature into a tree, pinning it in place with one of its massive arms. With the other, it grabbed the creature by the head and began twisting it. The creature struggled frantically. A crack filled the air and the creature slumped lifelessly. The elemental tossed the creature to the ground and stood there unmoving.

"I wonder if that creature was the cause of the blight," Aramis questioned.

"I suppose we shall find out soon," the druid answered.

"My throat is on fire. Is there a stream anywhere nearby?"

The druid pointed. "That way there's a shallow stream that flows all the way through the forest."

Aramis nodded and walked the direction the druid had indicated. He passed Kaldrick and motioned him to follow. "There's a stream this way if you're thirsty?"

Kaldrick followed him, his pace hindered somewhat by a slight limp. After a few hundred feet, Aramis heard a noise. It sounded like wind blowing through the treetops, but it turned out to be the stream. It flowed to the north, twisting and turning along the landscape. They stopped at the edge of the bank and Aramis knelt down. He splashed water onto his arms and washed the blood off. Then he cupped his hands together and dipped them into the water, quickly bringing them up to his mouth. He drank the water and immediately spit it out.

It was one of the foulest things he'd ever tasted. He spat several times, but it didn't help. He vomited into the stream. The taste was still in his mouth, but not as strong. He stared into the water and noticed a thin oily film floating on the water.

"What is it?" Kaldrick asked, stepping away from the water's edge.

"I think the stream has been affected by the blight," Aramis answered as he stood back up. "Gods that was nasty. Let's get back to the druids. Hopefully, they have better water in the village."

As they were approaching the ring of trees, he could hear shouting. He picked up his pace and realized it was the druids shouting. There were several of the gray-skinned creatures attacking them. The elemental was busy fighting three of them. Aramis looked back and saw Kaldrick was doing his best to keep up, but his limp was throwing him off. Kaldrick motioned for him to go ahead.

Aramis sprinted toward a group of creatures around one of the druids. He leaped into the air and stuck his leg out, slamming into one of the creatures with a jarring impact. The creature fell to the ground roughly. Aramis remembered he'd left his dagger in the back of the first creature and ran toward its body. One of the creatures stepped in front of him, stopping him short. It swung its arms at him, trying to rake him with its claws. He narrowly avoided the strikes and feigned going to the left, then went to the right and ran past the creature. He reached the body and yanked his dagger out of its back.

He turned to face the creature. It came at him quickly, clawing at him haphazardly. One of its claws gashed him on the shoulder. He jabbed the dagger into the creature's chest. On any normal man, it would have been a death blow, striking the heart. But the creature just roared in anger and grabbed onto his arm, dragging its claws across his flesh. Aramis's eyes widened as he saw how deep the creature cut him. He could see tendons and the white of his bone.

Fear engulfed him. He didn't think the tattoo would be able to heal that. As he stared at his arm, he saw the skin begin to close. Relief flooded him. Within seconds the wounds had closed fully, leaving only the wet blood on his skin. Aramis pulled the dagger free and stabbed it into the creature's neck. Black blood gushed from the cut in its chest and neck. His hand was covered in it. Jerking the blade out, he staggered backward out of the creature's reach. Though it had received two mortal wounds, it didn't appear to deter the thing at all. It came at him still.

Kaldrick rammed into the creature from the side, using his shoulder to knock it into a tree. Aramis ran over and together they punched, kicked and stabbed the creature until they were sure it was dead. Aramis turned to survey the scene around them, his breath coming in heaving gasps. The creatures had killed one of the druids. He lay in a pool of blood, covered in gashes. The three fighting the elemental were ripping pieces of its bark off. Aramis wasn't knowledgeable when it came to magic, but he was certain that the elemental wasn't going to last much longer.

He ran over to help the remaining druids who were being attacked. He glanced over to where the black grass was as he ran and saw five more of the creatures coming up out of the ground. At this rate, they would be quickly overrun and have to flee the area. How far would the creatures chase them? Would they follow them to the village?

Aramis growled in frustration. He was starting to feel helpless. All he had was a short dagger and it didn't do much damage to the creatures. He reached the druids and helped drive one of the creatures back, stabbing it several times with the dagger. Again, the wounds seemed not to faze it much. Aramis pushed the creature to the ground. He leaped on top of it, grabbed a rock from nearby, and bashed it into the creature's head over and over.

After it stopped moving, he dropped the rock and stood back up—only to be knocked painfully to the ground. More of the creatures leaped onto him. He was pinned down and could barely move. Intense fear gripped him as he realized he wasn't in control of the situation. Between flailing limbs, he saw more of the creatures running to join the fray from the direction of the black grass. They were sorely outnumbered now.

He struggled to move his arms. The weight of the creatures on him made it impossible. His heart was pounding in his chest. He could feel the creatures flaying his skin off. Everything seemed to slow down, but he didn't know if it was his imagination or from the loss of blood. He closed his eyes and prepared himself to die.

Summon your blade.

The words entered his mind, cutting through the chaos around him. Within seconds, he had an entire conversation with ... himself? His conscience? He didn't know and didn't have time to figure it out.

What?

Summon your blade.

What blade?

The Blade of Mordum.

How? I don't know what that is.

Focus.

On what?

On the power flowing through you.

It might drive me insane.

Insanity is better than death.

Is it?

You tell me.

Aramis snapped his eyes open. He had no idea what was happening inside his mind, but he focused on the power of the tattoo. A hissing sound filled the air and he noticed his hand was wet. He assumed it was blood. One of the creatures screeched wildly and flung itself off of him. He looked to his hand and saw a gleaming blade sword. Silver runes ran down the length of the blade. The tip of it was covered in a thick black liquid. He realized it was blood. Blood from the gray-skinned creature.

Using strength he didn't realize he had left, he drove the sword into the creatures atop him, slicing limbs off with ease. Within moments he was free and managed to get to his feet. His arms were healing, the deep wounds closing before his eyes. He looked at the carnage around him and was perfectly calm, perfectly in control of his thoughts.

The elemental lay defeated on the ground, looking like nothing more than a twisted tree. The druids were surrounded. They were chanting and holding their hands up. It looked like they had erected some sort of shield around themselves. It probably wouldn't hold for long. He could see sweat pouring down their faces and he knew they were exhausted.

Kaldrick. He found the man attempting to fight off two of the creatures. He was covered in blood, his own and that of the creatures. Aramis knew the man's strength was failing him by the way his body moved. Aramis walked toward the creatures and cut them down effortlessly; their heads rolling onto the ground, their black blood splattering the grass around him. Then he strode to the druids and began dispatching the creatures. They turned to fight him, but he was too quick; much quicker than they were. Limbs and heads flew in all directions as he dealt death with abandon.

He cleared the entire clearing of the creatures. The scene was so surreal; he almost didn't believe his eyes. Their bodies lay strewn all over. He saw the two druids who had been slain. So much death. The druids stopped their chanting and their shield faded from sight. Aramis glanced to where the creatures were coming up from the ground. He saw a hand rising from the hole. There were would be more, no doubt. Would they ever stop coming?

"Thank you," the druid said as he approached Aramis. "You saved our lives."

"Not all of them," Aramis said softly.

"Death comes to us all," he replied.

An idea formed in Aramis's mind. He had no way of knowing if it would work, but he had to try something to stop the hellish creatures from continuing their killing.

"Not always," Aramis said. He looked to Kaldrick as he limped over. "Stay with the druids until I return. I don't know how long it will be. Maybe hours, maybe days."

"Where are you going?" Kaldrick asked.

"Into the pit of Hell," Aramis answered. He walked toward the hole in the grass. Another one of the creatures was struggling to climb out. Aramis casually lopped off its head with a swing of his blade. He looked down at the hole, wondering what he might find below. He would never normally do something so insane. He held his sword up and studied the runes. It was Talvaarish for all he knew. Had summoning the blade given him the calmness he was experiencing? He didn't know.

He held his breath. And then he stepped down into Hell.

—Kaldrick

CHAPTER 9

Garrick mulled over the old woman's words as he sipped water from his canteen. They were still hard to believe. She had given them new canteens of water, and a new tent, before pushing on through the desert with her wooden cart.

He marveled at how she had survived out here, especially being blind. He looked at Kelvin. The man was ignoring him. Garrick sighed. At least the man wasn't intent on killing him now.

"I'm sorry," Garrick said.

Kelvin looked at him but remained silent.

"For not telling you."

Kelvin turned away.

"I'll explain everything if you let me. There is a reason I bear the Mark, and it is not what you likely think. I am not one of his mindless pawns."

"Tell me," Kelvin answered. He did not turn around.

"Very well. Please know that you will be the first

person to hear this. Not even my wife knows about this."

That seemed to get Kelvin's full attention, for he finally turned to face Garrick. Their eyes met and Garrick thought he sensed a change in Kelvin's eyes. A small change, but a change nonetheless.

"The Mark of Mordum can bring many different abilities, much like your goddess's blessing. It can also bring madness."

"I already know this," Kelvin said.

"Most people of faith do. However, you must be chosen by Mordum to receive the Mark. Usually, these people are already on a path of destruction. Murderers mostly. A few already claimed by madness and the occasional liar. By their actions, Mordum chooses them. It is rare that anyone would ever willingly choose to take the Mark."

Garrick took another sip of water.

"I was young …"

● ∞ ● ∞ ●

Garrick was up before sunrise. He dressed quietly in the dull reddish light provided by the hearth. His mother was still asleep and he didn't want to wake her. Stepping out of the house, he walked over to a barrel that held rainwater and splashed some on his face. He ran his wet hands through his tousled straight black hair several times. Checking his reflection on the water's surface, he decided his hair would just have to do.

The air still had a chill to it. He ran back into the cabin and grabbed a heavy cloak and threw it over his shoulders, then ran back outside. In his anxiousness, he almost forgot to close the door. He walked with a quick pace down the dirt road that winded through the small town. He could see puffs of his breath in the pre-dawn air.

The small town was quiet and still. The people were sleeping off the exhaustion from the previous day's work. Garrick had worked hard as well and was still tired, but his excitement at the return of his father and the other members of the town was too much to allow him to sleep. They had been gone a week, hunting and foraging in the woods for supplies to last the winter.

As the eldest of the town's kids, Garrick was naturally the leader. As such, his father charged him with helping to manage the town while the men were gone. That meant he was responsible for keeping the younger children in line and helping tend to the chores. Several of the cabins needed minor repairs and the perimeter of the town needed to be watched for bears and roaming packs of wolves. A lot of work, but Garrick didn't mind it. He was almost sixteen, which meant he was almost considered one of the men. Next year, when the men went out again, Garrick would be old enough to go with them.

"Where are you going?" a voice called out.

Startled, Garrick stopped and looked around. He realized quickly the voice was not directed at him. Pale candlelight flickered in the window of his friend's house. The voice belonged to Aela's mother.

"I'm going to greet father when he returns," Aela answered.

Garrick stood in the road and waited. They had planned to walk together to the top of the hill outside the town and watch for the men to return.

"It's dangerous out there," her mother said. "And the sun isn't up yet."

"I'll be fine," Aela protested. "The sun will be up soon and I'm not going alone. Garrick is waiting for me."

"Oooh," her mother said. "Go ahead, then. I don't want to hear about any kissing in the woods, though."

"Mother!" Aela screeched.

Garrick chuckled. A few years ago, he would have been disgusted at the thought of kissing a girl. That was something only adults did. Now, with manhood speedily approaching, he found that he liked looking at Aela more and more. She was younger than him, but she was blossoming into a beautiful woman. Though she was younger, she was slightly taller. He was barely above five feet and she was roughly four inches taller than him. He was dismayed when he didn't grow taller over the summer, but his father assured him that his height would come with time. Apparently, it ran in the family.

Aela stepped out of the house. The candlelight gave the appearance that she was glowing, like some otherworldly creature. She peered into the gloom. There was a gentleness to her, a softness that he had once viewed as weakness but now viewed as strangely distracting. Her hair was brown and smooth, thick enough to lose a hand in. It bounced around her shoulders with a charming ruggedness. Her eyes were a rich and clear blue, like two great lakes soaking in the world and reflecting her every mood. When her eyes showed sadness, he felt a sting in his heart. When they showed joy, his body danced on the clouds.

Her lips were big and full. Most of the boys in the town often made fun of Aela for her lips, saying that if she wanted to, she could whisper in her own ear. Garrick had no desire to taunt her when looking at her lips. He sensed their softness and found them so very inviting.

"I'll be home for lunch," Aela told her mother.

"The woods are dangerous in the dark," her mother warned, trying to dissuade her one last time.

"I'll be fine," Aela replied dismissively. Then she walked out to the road to meet Garrick.

"You're late," he said.

"I'm early," she insisted. "And I'm sleepy."

Garrick shrugged and led her with a swift pace. Despite her complaints, she kept pace with him and even passed him at one point. They left the town behind and began their ascent of the hill. Aela stopped and looked back, pointing to the sky.

"The stars," she said breathlessly.

Garrick turned to follow her gaze and smiled. Stretched across the sky were many different colored stars, all shining brightly against their black canvas. They stared in silence for a long while, neither speaking nor moving. Staring at the vastness of the sky, Garrick suddenly felt very small. The grandness of the stars overwhelmed him and though he felt small, he knew that he was a part of the vastness. A small, insignificant part, but a part nonetheless. He felt a strangeness in the atmosphere. It flooded him with heat and he vaguely felt the name "Mordum", though he didn't know why.

The sensation passed and Garrick turned to Aela. He was about to say something when he realized she was immersed in the same feeling as well. He suddenly felt very close to her, as though they were sharing a very private moment together.

He watched as she slowly drifted back to reality, the moment forever seared into Garrick's remembrance. He had a sudden urge to kiss her, but he resisted it. Barely.

"What?" she asked.

Garrick looked away, embarrassed by the feelings he had. Aela was his friend, of course, but she was a girl. Anything more than friendship was terrifying.

"Garrick?" she asked. "What's wrong?"

"Nothing," he replied abruptly. "Let's go. The sun will be up soon." He started up the hill at an intense pace, a few times even having to bend down and use his hands. He crunched through the thick layer of fallen leaves, the noise seeming louder than normal in the silence. Aela paused and watched him, confused at his abruptness. A smile found its way on her face and her cheeks began to blush. She suspected she knew the feelings Garrick was fighting. They were the same feelings she had fought earlier in the year. She had gained victory in that battle by accepting her feelings for Garrick. Every time she saw him, her stomach fluttered as though full of butterflies. She hoped he would find the same victory she had.

She caught up to him as they reached the peak of the hill. The valley below was dark and ominous, even though she had often ventured into the wooded place. The entire world seemed to be still. There were no birds chirping, no tree branches swaying, not even a hint of a breeze.

They sat down together, separated only by Garrick's confusion over his emotions. He tried hard to ignore her, but she stared at him intently which caused him to shift uncomfortably. She hid her amusement and looked away from him, down to the town behind them. She could pick her house out by the faint light in the window from the candle she had lit.

Looking back to the sky, she saw the stars were fading from sight. She could still make out some of the colors, but the odd feeling she had experienced was gone. As the sun rose, she began to see more of the town and even discern the different houses.

"They should be back today," Garrick said.

Aela hoped he was right. She missed her father when he was gone.

They sat in silence for several hours. The sun eventually brightened the world around them, making it easier to recognize their surroundings. In the valley below, Garrick could now make out the ancient trees—mostly evergreens and pines. The dew on the ground reflected the morning light in dazzling sparkles. A small stream could be seen meandering its way down into the valley and further out, further than Garrick could see. During the heat of the day, he knew he'd be tempted to strip off his clothes and go for a swim.

He saw Aela looking at him from the corner of her eyes and he turned away, blushing.

"From this height, we should spot them easily," Aela said.

Garrick was glad she wasn't staring at him openly now. He'd decided if she did it again, he would kiss her. Curse his inhibitions. He noticed movement down in the valley.

"There!" he said suddenly, pointing.

Aela looked to where he was pointing and could faintly see the men traveling through the forest. They jumped to their feet and began talking excitedly. The hunters would return with deer, elk and anything else they could catch. Garrick's patience quickly faded and he ran down the slope, trying to angle himself so that he'd intercept the returning men.

From the hilltop, the way down seemed easy and open. Going into the dense forest, Garrick quickly remembered how easy it could be to get lost. He looked back over his shoulder for Aela and saw she wasn't far behind him. He almost ran into a massive pine tree when he turned back around. As he zig-zagged through the tree line, he quickly lost Aela. They had to call out to one another for a short while in order to find each other. Then they argued for several minutes about which direction they should travel.

Being the natural leader, Garrick determined the best option would be to keep the sun at their backs since that's where it was when they were on the hilltop. Aela nodded her agreement, trusting in Garrick's instincts.

He wove his way through the thick trees, picking leaves off some of the trees as he walked. Autumn was well under way, and the leaves of the deciduous trees had already changed colors. Reds and oranges and yellows bathed everything around them. Garrick checked behind him frequently, keeping a closer eye on Aela. He picked up his pace when he heard the voices of the returning men.

Aela pushed past him suddenly, bursting into a clearing. The startled men drew their weapons, ready to defend themselves. Garrick stopped dead in his tracks and Aela screamed in surprise. The men began scolding them both, but Garrick barely heard them. Some of the men were carrying poles with animals strung on them.

His eyes went to each one, seeing a deer on one, an elk on another, and finally ... his eyes widened in surprise—and fear.

● ∞ ● ∞ ●

It was mid-afternoon by the time Garrick and Aela led the procession of hunters into the town. As the townspeople saw what the men had returned with, a crowd had quickly gathered and several people began asking questions. The reactions of the people ranged from curiosity to fear.

"Is it a goblin?" asked one woman.

Some of the younger children peered at the creature while they cowered behind their parents.

"I'm not sure," answered Kadin, Garrick's father.

Garrick had seen many things living on the edge of civilization, but he had never seen anything like this creature before. He had taken up a position next to the dead creature as though he were guarding it. He inspected it for the hundredth time, taking in every detail he could.

It was humanoid, but that was where the similarity ended. Its flesh was a distinct murky green color. He had noticed over the last few hours that the color was beginning to change, slowly fading to an ashen color. Its face was shaped like that of a man, but it had two elongated canines protruding from its mouth. A thin layer of black hair covered its entire body from the neck down. And it smelled. Badly.

"It's not a goblin," a man from the crowd answered. Garrick looked up to see the old man Len. The people moved out of his way as he limped forward. He stopped a few feet from the corpse and eyed it intensely.

"It's an orc," he said finally.

People began murmuring among themselves.

"How do you know that?" Kadin asked.

"I've seen them," Len answered and pat his leg. "This limp was caused by one of them."

Garrick turned his complete attention on Len, not wanting to miss any information. Normally he ignored the old man, just like most of the townsfolk. Now, however, he had everyone's attention.

"It was years ago. Myself and a few others were out by the Viss Mountains hunting. We had come across a group of them. Ugly brutes. They attacked us and we fought back. We outnumbered them, which is the only reason I'm standing here now. They were aggressive fighters and gave us a run for our gold if you know what I mean. Anyway, before they ran off, one of them struck me with its blade. Cut a deep gash in my leg. The other hunters had to carry me home. I thought for sure I was going to bleed to death."

Garrick recognized the look on his father's face as one of doubt. As other people chimed in with their own stories—rumors of orcs and goblins in other outlying towns, someone claiming to have been captured by a giant (and other less believable things)—Garrick began to realize they were just seeking attention.

Eventually, the interest died and the crowd dispersed. In less than half an hour, everyone was back to their normal duties. Garrick, however, was not to be deterred. He searched out Aela and gathered the children of the town. He took them out to the hilltop where he and Aela had spotted the hunters earlier that morning.

"Everyone has seen the orc?" he asked.

General agreement echoed back from the kids.

"Orcs are like deer. Where there's one, there's more."

Aela flashed Garrick a questioning glance as if to say "what are you talking about"?

"I heard Len talking about them with my father after everyone left. He says that these creatures are vicious. They travel in groups and they are always looking to kill humans."

Some of the children gasped in terror and looked around as if they would hide immediately. Others set their faces in scowls, looking prepared to fight.

"Since we have one of their dead friends, I think they'll come looking for its body."

"What does that have to do with us?" asked Aela.

Garrick tried not to be irritated. He thought that out of everyone, at least she would take his side in what he was going to propose.

"The adults are too busy preparing for the winter to worry about setting up guards to watch the borders of the town. So I have decided to step up to the task myself. I will coordinate everything, but I can't do this alone. I need help. From all of you."

Garrick got mixed reactions from the kids. Some of them were eager to volunteer, but most of them wanted nothing to do with it. In the end, he had only 5 kids volunteer, not including himself and Aela. After the kids had headed back to the town, Garrick began walking the perimeter of the town, doing some math in his head. Aela walked with him, though she remained silent.

"With only seven of us, we've got limited options. One of us can work all day, but that may not work well.

If they are on the north side of the city and the orcs come from the south, they would never know and the town would be overrun. I think our only option is for all of us to work every day. We'll be fairly spaced out, but it's all we can do."

"You do realize we aren't trained soldiers," Aela said.

Garrick nodded. "Yes. That's unfortunate, but we'll just have to make do with what we've got. There's an endless supply of wood around us, so we can sharpen some tree branches into spears."

Aela laughed.

Garrick stopped walking and turned to face her. She was starting to make him angry. "What is so funny?"

"You are," she answered. "You remind me of your father. Taking charge, planning everything. Have you spoken to him about this yet?"

"No," Garrick said, losing much of his confidence. "I wanted to have everything in line before I brought it to him. That way, he'd have no other option but to agree with it."

"I don't think that's how it works," she replied.

Garrick suddenly realized that they were alone. Not only that, but she was very close to him. Too close. He looked at her lips. They looked so soft, so …

"Garrick!"

He turned to see one of the kids, a boy named Kiernan, come running towards them. His pace slowed as he neared them and Garrick could see the boy was struggling to catch his breath.

"Your father is looking for you," he said. "He asked me to find you."

"Thanks for letting me know," Garrick replied. His eyes went back to Aela. She was smiling at him. "I'll see you later," he said. She nodded and he made his way back to the town. He found his father in the tavern seated with a few other adults next to the fireplace.

"Father," he said as he joined the group.

Kadin waved his hand and the other adults got up and went to another table. Garrick took one of their seats and looked his father in the eyes.

"I just heard an interesting rumor," Kadin said.

"What's that?"

"I heard you are trying to put together some guards."

The tone in his father's voice made him slump down in his chair. His father wasn't going to let him do it.

"I was going to have everything planned before I told you," Garrick said.

"That's commendable," Kadin replied, "but unnecessary. The leaders of the town have already discussed the matter. We will set the watch for the borders of the town."

"What about the things that need to be done for winter?" Garrick asked.

"We are going to take shifts. Some of us will do the work, some of us will guard the borders. We will do what we have to."

"I could—"

"No," Kadin said before Garrick could finish. "Preparing for winter is more important than playing soldier. We will likely freeze or starve to death before we'd be attacked by orcs."

Garrick bit his cheek angrily.

"I need to you help around the town like you normally do, but I need you to pick up more responsibility. With some of the adults on guard duty, we'll be shorthanded."

Garrick blinked slowly. He knew his father was wise, but he was tired of being seen as a child. He was almost a man and he wanted the adults of the town, especially his father, to see him that way. He decided he would do what his father asked without complaint. He would work extra hard and prove himself.

"Yes, father. I understand."

Kadin regarded his son thoughtfully. "Thank you. I know you likely don't agree, but I appreciate you doing it anyway."

Garrick gave a grudging nod of his head.

● ∞ ● ∞ ●

Eventually, the excitement died down. After a few weeks, with no sightings of any kind, the people of the town began to find the guard shifts unnecessary. Every day Garrick heard more and more complaints from the adults. And every day, when he asked his father for the responsibility of the watch instead of cabin repairs, the resistance in his voice faded.

Garrick had finished his work for the day and went to the tavern. When he walked in, he found his father standing at the bar talking with another of the town's leaders. They were deep in discussion when he walked up and tapped his father on the back.

Kadin turned around and smiled at his son.

"Father, I'd like to take over the watch today." He'd repeated the words so many times over the last few weeks, he'd almost gotten tired of saying them.

"Done," his father said.

Garrick's face lit up in surprise. He knew his father was becoming less resistance to the idea, but he was still shocked when his father agreed.

"Really?" Garrick asked.

"Yes, really." Kadin handed him a parchment with a crude drawing of the town on it. His father pointed to various points. "This is where we're currently keeping a watch. You should keep to these areas. The adults will no longer take shifts after today, so you are limited to whoever volunteers from the children. Make sure everyone is well armed. Speaking of," his father paused as he unwrapped something on the bar, "take this."

He handed Garrick the family sword. Garrick swelled with pride and gingerly took the sword from his father. It was old. The blade had specks of rust on it and several notches along the edges, but it was a *sword*.

"I expect a daily report from you," Kadin said sternly. He knew that his son desperately wanted to be seen as a man. If he acted as though this was not a serious matter, it would crush something in his son. He would never forgive himself if he did that.

"Yes, father." Garrick raced off to gather his "soldiers".

"Do you think that's a good idea?" the man at the bar asked.

"Why not?" Kadin answered. "He finds value in protecting others."

"I mean letting the children roam about the forest. It's dangerous out there."

"It can be. If the orcs come, they'll be safer in the woods than they will be in the town. We have no defenses. No wall to hide behind. We have more farming tools than we do weapons."

"True."

"But let's be serious. Orcs attacking the town?" Kadin snorted.

"Lest you've forgotten, we encountered a band of them while we were hunting."

"I know, but that was thirty miles from here. There've been no reports from any of the other towns about anything out of the ordinary. I think it was a chance meeting out in the wilds."

The other man shrugged.

● ∞ ● ∞ ●

The patrol began the next day, with the five volunteers, Aela, and himself walking the edges of the town's borders. While the majority of the adults stopped taking shifts, there were two teenagers, older than Garrick, who went deeper into the woods each day to do their own patrol.

Garrick knew them fairly well and knew that although the two were entrusted with the more important patrol sweep, his group was just as important. If the two caught sight of the orcs, they would rush to the border and find Garrick, who would then alert the town. Garrick knew that were that to happen, he'd be considered a hero.

He didn't take charge of the guard duties for that reason, however. He wanted to make sure everyone was safe. In order to ensure that, he needed to be in charge. He needed to be the one to make decisions, quick decisions, that would help to avoid danger to the people of the town. His spirit was soaring as he was one step closer to being considered a man.

As the days came and went, the weather began to change. Colder winds began to blow in from the south, causing the patrol to have to end earlier in the evening. One of the boys in his group was eight and his mother complained incessantly if he wasn't back before dusk. Garrick knew their time was growing short, but he didn't want to acknowledge it.

Two weeks passed by uneventfully. The patrol had dropped to three, including Aela and himself. Garrick kept at it, covering as much of the borders as he could by himself when Aela had to go home. Once Aela was no longer able to patrol with him, there would be no point and he knew his father would call upon him to start helping around the town again. Winter was almost on them and there was still much to do.

"It's time for me to get home," Kiernan said. His

words broke Garrick's contemplations. He waved the boy off.

Garrick stabbed his sword forcefully into the ground.

"What's wrong?" Aela asked.

"What do you mean?" he replied.

Aela recognized the frustration in his voice, though he made an attempt to seem nonchalant. She stepped closer to him.

"Their parents are calling them home because no orcs have been seen," Aela said gently. "That's a good thing."

Garrick rolled his eyes.

"Do you disagree? Would it be better for orcs to overrun our town and likely kill everyone?" She realized immediately that she had wounded his pride. He likely hadn't thought of that, and even if he had, what could a small band of kids do to defend against orcs?

"I'm sorry, I didn't mean that what we've been doing is unimportant. It is. But maybe it is better that we patrol and find nothing. Winter is setting in. Do you know how hard it would be to defend a town that is unprepared for the cold?"

"Do you?" Garrick retorted.

"No," Aela answered without pause. "But my father does. And so does yours. They have enough to worry about without the threat of orcs."

Garrick sighed. He knew she was right, of course. She was always the sensible one. He didn't really know what he'd expected. Eventually, it would be too cold to patrol. Once the snow began to fall, it would be even less likely that orcs would come this far.

"I suppose you are right," Garrick conceded.

Aela reached out hesitantly and grabbed his chin in her hand, turning his head to face her. "You are a natural leader," she said softly. "You will do great things."

"I—"

She stopped him from speaking by covering his mouth with her hand. It was then that Garrick realized how close they were. Her face was inches from his. He was suddenly hot. He could feel his skin flush with heat. His heart started beating fast.

Aela closed the gap and moved her hand, pressing her lips against his. She *kissed* him. His eyes widened in surprise, then fear, then pleasure. He almost pushed her away. A year ago, he would have. Not now. He realized that he was ready for it now. Did she know he was ready? She must have. They'd spent the majority of the day together for the last few weeks. She knew him better than anyone else. She knew him better than he knew himself some days.

He slowly slid his arms around her and pulled her closer. She pressed against him and he could feel the curves of her body. He experienced a moment of panic. He didn't know where he should put his hands, or better yet, where he shouldn't put his hands. All he knew was that he didn't want the kiss to end and that he wanted something more, but he didn't know what that might be. He realized at that moment that he loved Aela.

That thought scared him and he broke away to catch his breath. She stared at him, smiling brightly. He stared back at her, into her eyes and the fear melted away. Garrick leaned toward her, his hands gently touching her face, and kissed her. She pushed herself against him. Their clothes were suddenly a hindrance. Garrick moved his hands from her face to her neck, caressing her soft skin, before moving down her arms and onto her hips. The kiss became less gentle and more urgent. His hand brushed the outside of her thigh and she opened her mouth, giving a soft moan. She surprised him when her tongue touched his lips. It was soft, inviting him …

And then the moment was destroyed by a horrified scream. The two broke apart, startled. Garrick turned toward the town. Smoke was rising from one of the buildings and countless forms were rushing into the town.

Orcs.

Thousands of orcs. They had finally come.

—Jerik

CHAPTER 10

An acrid smell filled Aramis's nostrils. He coughed involuntarily, trying not to breathe through his nose. Everything around him seemed to ripple, as though he were looking at a mirage from far away. It made his eyes water if he stared in one spot for too long. And everything was gray. Not that there was much to see. A barren landscape stretched endlessly before him in all directions.

There was no plant life, no trees, nothing. He thought the ground was dirt until he knelt down and grabbed a handful of it. It was a thick powdery substance. He brushed it off on his pant leg. He looked up and surveyed what he assumed was the sky. It was hard to tell the ground from the sky, for each one was the same dull gray color. Aramis didn't see any of the creatures. He found that odd, as they had been pouring through the hole above ground.

Where did they come from? He wondered.

His words echoed across the landscape. The sound startled him. He hadn't spoken the words out loud, yet they were audible. He stood in silence and eventually the echo faded. Guessing as to which way was North, he started walking. His steps caused the dusty ground to sink beneath his feet and send small clouds of the stuff into the air.

The air still smelled, but he was getting acclimated to it. He considered turning back after several minutes but quickly discarded the thought. He needed to find the source of the blight—of the creatures—and destroy it. He trudged on for what felt like hours. The sun wasn't visible, but the temperature was uncomfortably warm. He wasn't sweating though, which was a dramatic difference from the forest. The air above was humid and made him sweat between his legs, which gave him a rash.

He saw something ahead. At first, he thought it was his imagination. But as he got closer, he realized that the tower was very real. At least a hundred of the gray-skinned creatures stood guard, an equal number on either side. He halted his approach and brought his sword up defensively. The creatures had to have seen him by now, but they weren't moving. He resumed walking toward the tower but kept his pace slow, watching the creatures intently.

The tower wasn't enormous. Aramis guessed it to be about three stories high. It was simple in design and there were windows on each level. He stopped a hundred feet from the tower. The creatures still hadn't budged.

"Come in," a heavy voice boomed from the tower.

Aramis shied back a few steps. The voice was loud and piercing. The tattoo on his arm began to burn. He rubbed it with the hilt of his sword and slowly made his way closer. In the center of the tower was a doorway with no doors. He hesitated at the threshold of the doorway for a moment, glancing to the creatures. They paid him no attention, so he stepped inside. Aramis touched the surface of one of the walls. It was made of the same gray powder as the ground, but it had been hardened and was sturdy.

A single, plain staircase wound its way upward along the wall. The frames where the windows were had no glass and was open to the air outside. Aramis followed the stairs with his eyes, but he couldn't see where they led. There was nothing else of note. He began climbing the stairs. By the time he reached the top, his legs muscles were burning fiercely. Where the stairs ended there was a small platform. He walked across the landing and through a doorway.

Aramis entered a large circular room. At the back of the room stood an upraised throne on a large dais. At the end of each armrest was a human skull. And seated on the throne was an enormous beast. Aramis felt the hairs of his neck stand on end at the sight of it. He'd never seen anything like it, not even in his nightmares.

The beast's head was that of a large cat he'd only seen pictures of. Its upper body was massive and muscular and reminded Aramis of a bull. Its arms ran down the length of the armrests and it had human hands. The lower body was feathered and its feet had talons several inches long, all of them razor sharp.

"Kneel, servant of Mordum."

The voice of the beast was deafening and shook the foundation of the tower. Despite his fear, Aramis did not bow. He merely stood staring at the dreadful thing before him. How could something like that even exist?

The beast stood up and Aramis involuntarily dropped to his knees, his sword clattered onto the floor. Its very appearance exuded a tremendous power. The beast's talons clacked against the floor as it walked toward him. It took everything he had to keep his bladder from despoiling his pants. The beast towered over him, making him feel extremely small. It lowered its head and sniffed his hair, then snorted. The beast's breath was hot and putrid.

"What has brought you to my domain? Is it time?"

"Time f-for w-what?" Aramis asked haltingly.

"Is it time for Mordum to release me onto the world? My slaves have infected the home of the druids as he commanded. Is it time now for my wrath to be poured out?"

Aramis could only shake his head in reply. The beast growled.

"Then why are you here, servant?"

Aramis couldn't speak. His mind screamed the response: *I'm here to stop the infection of the forest!* The words echoed within the tower as if he spoke them aloud. The beast laughed. It was a terrible sound and made Aramis tremble. It leaned down and sniffed at him again, longer this time. The beast's pupils turned to slits.

"You haven't submitted to the Mark yet," it said slowly. Realization must have dawned on the beast. *"Crafty mortal. Foolish mortal."*

The beast circled around Aramis, eyeing him with its feline gaze. Aramis had never even heard of such a creature. *Mind over body*, he reminded himself. If he could focus his mind, then he could control his body. He looked away from the creature and down at his sword. He hadn't even realized he'd dropped it. The creature continued to stalk around him.

The creature said he unleashed the plague on the forest.

Aramis steeled his nerves. He grabbed his sword and stood up, then turned to face the creature. He almost lost control of his mind as fear spread through his body. He knew the creature could tear him limb from limb without a second thought. He brought the blade up and stepped toward the beast, quickly swinging the blade in a horizontal strike.

The creature was faster than he expected and it back stepped the swing easily. It laughed and lashed out at him with its clawed leg. The talons cut deep gashes along his leg. Aramis cried out in pain and staggered back. He tried not to put weight on it. The tattoo on his arm itched and he watched as the gashes healed before his eyes. He turned his attention back to the creature.

"That's an interesting talent you've got. I wonder if it will reattach your head to your body?"

The creature roared savagely and came at him full speed. Aramis tried to bring his sword up, but the beast crashed into him and they tumbled to the floor. His hand slipped from the hilt of his blade and he dropped it again. The creature wrapped one of his large human hands around Aramis's neck and began squeezing.

Aramis felt his windpipe crush under the power of the creature. His eyes bulged wide from both the pain and the lack of oxygen. He experienced an intense fear as he didn't feel the power of the tattoo healing him. He desperately tried to pull the creature's hand away. It was futile. His body started to twitch spasmodically.

Your dagger.

The same subconscious voice he'd heard earlier. His vision was beginning to blur and he was having trouble understanding what was happening. Without thinking, his right hand retrieved the rusty dagger from his waist. With his last bit of energy, he tried to stab the creature in the chest. He lost all feeling in his body.

His vision went black. He couldn't hear anything. Aramis knew he was dead. Yet if he was dead, how was he still able to think? And then his mind went blank.

● ∞ ● ∞ ●

Aramis groggily opened his eyes. He lay there unsure of where he was. His head was throbbing with annoying pain. Sitting up took an enormous effort. As soon as he saw his surroundings, everything came flooding back to him. The creature that had tried to kill him was lying slumped against the wall in a pool of blood.

At least, he assumed it was blood. It wasn't red like his own. It was black. Just like the gray-skinned creatures he'd fought in the forest. He looked around, trying to determine what or who might have killed the beast. There was no evidence of anyone else having been in the room. His dagger lay next to him. It was covered in the same black blood.

He sheathed the dagger back at his waist and stood up, making a mental note that he'd need to clean the dagger when he got out from … wherever he was. His sword lay a few feet away. He wondered if he had to will the sword to disappear to make it go back to wherever he had summoned it from. He heard footsteps coming from outside the room. Several pairs of footsteps, judging by the sound. Aramis forced himself onto his feet. Other than the minor headache and feeling exhausted, he was unscathed.

Just as he picked up his sword from the floor, a group of the gray-skinned creatures entered the room. They stopped and looked from the dead creature to Aramis, then back to the creature. One of them shrieked. The sound pierced Aramis's skull painfully. He clenched his eyes shut and shook his head. When the creature stopped, Aramis realized they were all staring at him. And then he heard more footsteps, only this time they sounded like they were running.

Aramis considered his options quickly. They were coming in the door he entered, so he couldn't go that way. He could try fighting his way out, but it didn't seem likely he could defeat an army of the creatures.

While he may not die, it was possible they could overpower him and keep him from escaping. Aramis didn't like the idea of spending the rest of his life as a prisoner.

He glanced around the room. There was only one option. He ran towards one of the windows and jumped. As he plummeted toward the ground, he realized he was a little higher above the ground than he thought. Apparently, the tower was higher up than it looked from outside. He landed onto the powdery ground with a grunt and narrowly avoided injuring himself with his own sword.

Most of the creatures were pouring into the tower, but some of them noticed him. They ran towards him, shrieking wildly. Aramis struggled momentarily to dismiss his blade. He had no idea what he was doing. Finally, the air hissed as the blade disappeared in a swirl of mist. He hoped he could get out of this place the way he had entered it. He sprinted in the directions he'd come from, dodging past the creatures as they neared him.

They chased after him. He looked over his shoulder and saw that the other creatures had realized he was fleeing and they began pouring out of the tower. Some of them stormed out of the doorway, and others leaped from the windows. It was a scary sight. Aramis focused on the power flowing through him from the tattoo and fell into it.

The landscape blurred around him as he ran with increased speed. The creatures were far behind him now, but they were still chasing him. As long as he could get to the portal and get out, he would be fine. He ran for several minutes before he slowed his pace and forced himself out of the tattoo's power. Looking around, he couldn't tell where the portal was that he entered from. The gray landscape all looked the same.

He felt like he was walking in circles. It wouldn't be

long before the creatures caught up to him. Aramis was starting to get worried. What if he couldn't get out of this place? He growled in frustration and continued looking for anything that was different. And then he found a single leaf. He knelt down and examined it. It looked like the leaves from the forest. The portal had to be close. He looked straight up and saw a small black spot above him.

Aramis assumed it must be the portal. The grass in the forest had been black. The only problem he had now was how to reach it. It swirled about three feet above him. He wracked his brain for ideas. Not far in the distance, he could see the creatures coming.

He only had one idea. And it had to work. He summoned his sword and stabbed it into the ground. It sunk a foot deep. He shook his head, hoping it was long enough. Aramis placed one foot on the cross guard of the hilt and used it to jump into the air. His hand missed the portal by mere inches. He was so close. He did it again, trying to jump higher. Again, he missed by only a few inches. He had enough time to try once more before the creatures were on him.

He took a few steps back and got a running start, then stepped onto the cross guard and leaped into the air. The fingertips of his right hand made it into the portal. Aramis didn't know what he was touching, but he gripped it with all his might. It was soft and damp. As he hung there in the air, he guessed he was holding onto dirt or wet grass. He honestly wasn't sure which. The creatures were swarming below him, trying to grab his dangling legs.

Aramis moved his feet around, trying to stay out of their reach. He dismissed his sword so the creatures couldn't use it against him. He lifted his other arm and reached into the portal. With both hands gripped firmly, he tried to lift himself up. His arms were burning and his hands were cramping up. He considered himself to be in fit shape, but he simply couldn't lift himself. He started to laugh softly at the futility of his situation. Not much longer and he would lose his grip and fall.

He focused his mind on the tattoo. He could feel its power pulsing. He closed his eyes and tried to force his will onto the power. His mind struggled against the power as he tried to bend it to his will. Aramis wanted the strength to lift himself up. He focused only on that thought, putting everything he had into it. The tattoo began to itch. He felt a renewed feeling enter his body. He tried again to lift himself out of the portal. His progress was slow but steady.

Finally, he pulled himself completely out of the portal and threw himself onto the ground beside it. He released the power and immediately felt extremely drained. Every muscle in his body burned. He could feel his arms trembling. Looking around, he saw he had escaped back into the forest. He laughed again, this time in relief. No one would ever believe where he'd been or what he'd done. His head rolled weakly to look at the portal. He wondered when it would close.

What if it doesn't? he thought. Dread filled him as he entertained the thought. What if the portal didn't close and the creatures started coming out of it again? He had to find a way to close it; but how? He could barely move. He was utterly exhausted. He fought a losing battle to keep his eyes open.

No.

Aramis would not pass out before he closed the portal. He immersed himself into the power of the tattoo once more. It was harder this time. The power was like a river flowing away from him. He tried to catch it, but he was too slow, too sluggish. He wrestled against the impending darkness of sleep and tried to grab the power.

He felt it faintly slip through his fingers. He tried

harder, using what he had left in him. He managed to get a weak hold on it. He bent the power to his will and forced it to close the portal. He felt like he was struggling with an immovable wall. The portal wouldn't budge. Aramis was losing control of the power again. He could feel it slipping from his hands.

Reaching deep inside, he grabbed hold of his own spirit and fed it into his willpower. The portal grew smaller. It was only a fraction of a movement, but it gave him the hope he needed that he could close it completely. Something latched onto his physical arm. It startled him and almost broke his concentration. He pulled more from his spirit and forced the portal closed. He heard a pain filled yelp as it shut completely. Releasing the power of the tattoo, he pulled more of his spirit and fed it into his body to give him strength.

He opened his eyes and found everything was blurred. He blinked several times until his surroundings came into focus. He still felt weak. And he felt … different. It wasn't a bad feeling, but it wasn't good either. He felt almost as if he were missing something. Some part of him on the inside. He shrugged the feeling away and forced himself to get up. He could rest later. Glancing around the clearing, he didn't see Kaldrick or the druids. They had probably gone back to the village.

Aramis looked to where the portal had been. The grass was a dull gray color. Laying in the center of the circle was part of one of the creature's arms. One of them had almost escaped before he closed it. He rubbed his face tiredly and made his way to the trail that led to the druid village. He couldn't wait to get some sleep.

"Mordum demands everything."

—Garrick

CHAPTER 11

Adamar stood in front of his bedroom window, staring out at the sprawling city of Oakhaven. He was feeling good today despite the previous night's mishap. Watching the people below go about their daily lives, he told himself that they were beginning to love him.

He'd been hard on everyone initially, but for good reason. They were used to the weakness of his father. The man had essentially let the nobles run the kingdom. They needed to see that he was not weak like his father. And so he had been forceful with many of the nobles to show his dominance.

He didn't turn around when he heard the servants enter his chamber. They were there to set up his extravagant breakfast. Now that he was king, he dined on sumptuous food, had more gold than he could spend, and lived in a magnificent castle. He had Mordum's favor, his enemies feared him, and soon his god would bless him with the Mark. All he needed now was a wife, and he already had someone in mind.

Turning from the window, he walked over to the table the servants had set. Plump grapes—both green and purple—several different kinds of cheese, and fresh bread were all arranged in a neat pattern. Grabbing a few of the grapes, which had conveniently been pulled from the stems already, he popped them into his mouth. As he chewed them, he found they were very juicy and sweet with only a slight tang.

In the corner of his eye, he could see one of his templar guards standing in the shadows near the door. He motioned to the table.

"Hungry?"

The man shook his head. Adamar shrugged and ate a few more grapes. At first, he'd thought it odd that his guards rarely spoke, but as the years had passed he had gotten used to it. They'd been his guards since the day he accepted Mordum's offer. He shook his head thinking back on that day. It seemed like ages had passed since then, and at the same time, it felt like it was only a few days ago.

Pouring himself a glass of sweet honey wine, he sniffed the expensive liquid and enjoyed the taste on his tongue after he drank some. Walking back over to the window, he continued gazing out at the city as he sipped the wine. A servant came in and laid his clothes out on the bed before quietly excusing herself. He finished off the wine and then changed his clothes.

Grabbing a robe from the closet, Adamar draped it over his clothes. It was white trimmed in gold. And it was long, almost brushing the floor. In the center, where his back was, the Oaktree symbol of his kingdom was stitched in a vibrant blue. He checked his appearance in a mirror and then left the room, striding through the hall.

Servants and soldiers alike averted their eyes as they passed him. He smirked. Whether it was out of reverence for him or fear of his guards, he didn't know. Either way, they were honoring Mordum whether they knew it or not. He left the main keep and turned his direction toward the home of one of the nobles. As he got close, he was greeted by servants. They threw rose petals on the ground in front of him as he walked. The nobleman met him at the edge of the property.

"King Adamar!" he hailed as he bowed low.

"Lord Bavol," Adamar returned.

"I see you've come to call on me?"

"Of a sort," Adamar said. "I've come to talk to you about your daughter."

Bavol's face, for just a split second, betrayed him. Adamar made a mental note of it for later.

"My daughter?" Bavol asked, smiling widely.

"Yes. I am in need of a wife, and I have seen her around the court. She is a beautiful creature. She hasn't been promised to anyone, has she?"

"Uh, no. No, my lord, she hasn't."

Adamar smiled. "Good. Is the lady home?"

"I'm afraid not, m'Lord. She's out gallivanting as women do. I'm sure you know what I mean. Anyway, I will let her know you came to see her."

Adamar nodded, studying the man. He decided he didn't like the man. He'd need to be replaced, preferably with someone more willing to hide his emotions. Yes, he would definitely need to be replaced.

"I expect to be married at the end of the week," Adamar informed him. "An escort will be here then to bring her to the castle."

Bavol bowed low in subservience. Adamar eyed the nobleman's property and then turned and left.

● ∞ ● ∞ ●

After Adamar left, Lord Bavol glanced down both directions of the street and retreated into his home. He ordered the servants to start packing up the house. When they stared at him in confusion, he waved them off.

"Hannah!" he called out. "Hannah!"

His daughter came down the stairs from the second floor.

"Yes, father?"

"It's time," he said.

Her face and shoulders slumped.

"Now?"

"Immediately," he answered. "Adamar came calling for you. I told him you weren't here, but he's made his intent to take you as his wife quite clear."

"Has there been any word from Aramis?" she asked hopefully.

"Not yet," he answered.

"It's been months," she said, her words hinting at what they both feared.

"I know, but do not worry about such things. We have to get somewhere safe."

She nodded and ran back up the stairs.

Bavol called for a servant. He had the woman pen a letter, dictating to her what he wanted it to say. He would have written it himself, but he was too nervous to keep his hands steady. After the letter was finished, he called for a runner.

"Take this letter to the king of Talvaard," he instructed.

"My lord?" the man asked.

"You heard me. Guard this letter with your life. You must deliver it to the king himself. I do not expect a reply, but if he gives you one, don't bring it here. Go to the cabin. You remember where it is?"

The man nodded.

"Good. We'll be there until I feel it is safe enough to come back here. I cannot stress enough the importance of this letter's delivery."

"I will deliver it," the man answered.

"Do not fail," Bavol said.

The man bowed low, tucked the letter in his shirt, and sprinted off.

"For the sake of the kingdom, do not fail," Bavol whispered to himself.

● ∞ ● ∞ ●

Adamar was interrupted by a knock on his door later that night. In the middle of undressing, he waved to the guard by the door. He opened it and a soldier entered and bowed low.

"What is it?" Adamar asked though he was certain he knew the answer.

"Lord Bavol has left the city."

Adamar snorted.

"Coward. No matter. Are they being followed?"

"Yes, my lord. His daughter is also with him."

"And a liar. Lord Bavol is a disgrace to this kingdom. He will have to be dealt with."

"Your orders, my lord?"

"Nothing for now. Inform me as soon as you discover where he's going."

The soldier bowed again and left.

"Why do men run from their fate?" he asked aloud.

As expected, neither of his guards answered. Pushing the thought from his mind, he made his way over to the bed.

"What do you think?" he asked.

The sheets moved and two women looked up at him questioningly.

"Why do men run from their fate?" he repeated.

"Perhaps they can't … handle it," one of them said seductively, arching her brow.

Adamar smiled at her.

"Can you handle it?" he asked as he climbed into the bed.

"Let's find out," she purred.

"Loss is always a heavy burden."

—Jovanna

CHAPTER 12

"I'm sorry to hear that," Kelvin said quietly. "I never knew any of that."

Garrick nodded. "It was a long time ago."

"You still haven't told me how you got the Mark."

"I'm leading up to it. Once I saw the orcs pouring into the city, I could only think of one thing."

● ∞ ● ∞ ●

Aela screamed and sprinted down the hill toward the town. Garrick would have stopped her, but he was frozen with fear. His mind told him to do something, but he didn't know what to do. He had never been in battle. He'd never even seen a battle.

Somehow he gained control of his mind and followed Aela's path down the hill. Halfway down a large orc intercepted him. The ugly creature raised a crudely made spear. Garrick tried to slow his pace and almost tripped.

He lifted the sword his father had given him and rolled his wrist, causing the blade to move in a circular motion and knock the spear out wide.

As Garrick ran past the orc, he swung the sword up and around, turning himself in a complete circle, and slammed the blade against the orc's head. The creature jerked awkwardly and slumped to the ground. Garrick was surprised how easy it was to kill the thing. He continued running down the hill and into the town. Chaos was everywhere. Many of the townspeople were dead, lying broken and bloody in the streets.

Garrick looked frantically for his parents. He ran to a spot between two houses, slipped into the small space, and peered around the corners. There were no defenses, so the orcs had taken the entire town before the people were even aware of what happened. Sounds of fighting drew his attention and he saw his father and several others had formed a defensive ring around some of the women and children.

They were surrounded by orcs. Garrick almost considered joining them, but he knew it was a lost cause. The orcs were making short work of the men. Garrick watched in horror as one of the orcs stabbed forward with a spear, striking his father in the chest. Blood poured freely from the wound when the orc pulled the spear back.

Garrick turned his head, not wanting to believe what he saw. Soon after, the screams of the women and children filled the air and he knew that the men had fallen. He needed to escape the town, but he also wanted to find Aela. She was likely dead, but he had to hope for something good. He made his way cautiously through the town, running and ducking into hiding spots wherever he could.

As he neared Aela's home, he recognized the shouting of her mother's voice. Hope filled him and he ran to the house, only to find three orcs ripping Aela's mother to pieces. He gagged as one of them ripped her arm off. He turned to flee and saw Aela struggling against a pair of orcs. Fighting to ignore his fear, he ran over to help her. Before he could reach her, one of the orcs grabbed her by the hair, jerked her head back, and stabbed her in the throat with a wicked looking dagger.

"No!" he screamed.

The orcs turned their attention toward him. They ran at him, hollering something in their guttural language he didn't understand. His parents were dead, and now his friend. What else did he have in the world to live for? He wanted to throw his sword down and let them kill him. He wanted to die.

But his instinct for self-preservation wouldn't allow him to. Garrick brought his sword up and tried to knock away their spears. He'd never been trained with a sword though, and his attempts were weak. The orcs quickly outmaneuvered him and one of them struck him in the face with the butt of his spear.

Garrick reeled backward and landed on his back. He could feel the warm flow of blood pouring from his nose. His vision was blurred from the tears in his eyes. He blinked rapidly, trying to clear them. His hands scrabbled around desperately trying to find the hilt of his sword, but it eluded him. His hand came to rest on a rock, and he gripped it tightly.

One of the orcs stepped over him and leaned down. Its foul breath reminded him of a long-dead animal he had once encountered in the woods. Drops of saliva dripped from its mouth, landing on his neck. He gritted his teeth and swung as hard as he could. The rock in his hand connected solidly with the orc's temple. A loud *crack* sounded and the orc staggered back, howling in pain and outrage. Garrick scrambled to his feet and saw his sword. It was at the feet of the second orc, who was coming right at him.

Garrick grabbed the first orc's spear and swung wildly, smacking the orc in the head and neck several times. The creature growled at him. Garrick realized he was probably annoying it more than he was hurting it. He tried to stab the tip of the spear into the orc, but it was wearing what appeared to be armor made of bone. It kept the spear tip from doing any damage.

The orc grabbed hold of the spear and yanked it from him. Garrick let go of the weapon and sprinted past the creature, sweeping the sword up quickly. The first orc had recovered from his hit and was also coming at him now. Garrick's nose was still bleeding and he was starting to feel lightheaded. It was an odd feeling. He shook his head, hoping to stop his sight from fading. He had nothing left to lose.

He charged the two orcs, hacking and slashing haphazardly. They didn't seem too worried about him and didn't put up much of a defense. He was quickly losing his strength and energy. Changing tactics, he swung the sword low and tried to take out their legs. He struck one of them hard, but the dull blade didn't even break the skin. It still caused a considerable amount of pain, for the orc howled in agony. The other orc circled around behind Garrick. He was trapped between the two creatures with nowhere to go.

Something inside—some instinct—told him to drop down. He threw himself to the ground immediately. Above him, a spear from one orc struck the other. Where Garrick lacked the strength to penetrate the orc's bone armor, the first orc's force was enough to not only puncture it but also to stab straight through the second orc's flesh and out its back.

The creature dropped to the ground, dead. The other orc shouted something that Garrick assumed was a curse. The orc kicked him hard in the back. Garrick slammed into the ground face first. He grunted from the impact and rolled onto his back. The orc had its dagger gripped tightly and lunged toward him. Without thinking, Garrick raised up his sword. He missed the creature's chest and abdomen, but the orc's groin became impaled on the blade.

An unearthly cry of pain filled the air that made Garrick shudder. The fight was gone from the creature as it held itself and dropped to its knees. Garrick wanted to flee, but he knew it would be foolish to leave without his blade. He risked a look around. The entire town was ablaze. Dead bodies, both orc and human, littered the ground. The screams had all but stopped completely. No other orcs had noticed him yet, but he knew it was only a matter of time.

He kicked the orc in the face and felt the crunch of bone beneath his foot. The creature fell onto its back and Garrick grabbed the hilt of his sword and yanked the blade free. To his surprise, the orc was still alive. He considered killing the creature but instead started running for the tree line. He made it without being seen, at least as far as he knew.

As he ran, he ripped a piece of cloth from his shirt, rolled it up and stuffed it into his nostrils. He ran until the town was far behind him and his legs threatened to give out, then he stopped his frantic pace and slowed to a walk, continuously looking over his shoulder to see if he had been followed. He was exhausted. And thirsty. Those needs tugged at the edge of his mind, but they were kept at bay by the burning of his lungs and muscles.

His breath came in short, quick gasps. He was drenched in sweat and could feel it dripping down his skin. The sun was beginning to descend. Somehow he was aware of the fact that night was approaching and he needed to find shelter. He needed water too. Ahead, he thought he saw the outline of a cave among the trees. He angled his steps toward it and collapsed at the entrance.

It wasn't a cave at all. It was a door. He laid down on the soft ground and stared at the huge wooden door. He was going to pass out. He could feel it coming. His vision began swimming. The last thing he remembered before he fell into darkness was a large cross. Upside down.

● ∞ ● ∞ ●

Garrick awoke with a pounding headache.

He lay still for a moment, trying to figure out where he was. Shafts of starlight peeked down at him through the foliage above. Shakily, he rose to his feet. A massive wooden door stood before him. It seemed to cover the entrance of a cave and was hidden by the surrounding trees. Two torches, placed on either side of the door, burned low.

He looked back and tried to remember how he got there. In a whirlwind, it all came back to him. He vomited. Somewhat. There wasn't much to come up. Garrick became acutely aware of his hunger and thirst. Seeing no other options, he knocked on the door. It was sturdy and his knock barely made a sound. He knocked harder, pounding his fist on the wood as hard as he could. Throbbing pain filled his hand. He was about to kick the door when it opened suddenly. Not all the way. Just a crack. Enough that he was able to push it open.

Thoughts of his ransacked town and dead parents could not hold his mind as he crossed the threshold from the forest into a grand entrance hall. He gaped in disbelief.

The hall was enormous. Torches spaced the wall at regular intervals, providing enough light to see the splendor around him. High above, the ceiling was shrouded in darkness. He had never seen anything so spacious in his life. The effort to create such a wonder boggled his imagination.

Magnificent tapestries lined the walls between the torches, depicting scenes of battles between armored knights—some in silver, others in black. The details woven into the fabric were staggering. Hundreds of colors captured his eyes, unfurling stories he had never heard. Racks of weapons and suits of armor were placed below the torches, the light seeming to dance off their metal surfaces.

Garrick walked slowly down the hall, his attention diverted in every direction. At the end of the hall was a huge rectangular table. His house was smaller than the table was long, making him wonder who had taken the time to craft it. Certainly, no mortal hands had any part of it.

At the very end of the table stood a tall chair. As he walked nearer, he realized there was a figure sitting in it.

"I'm sorry for coming in uninvited," Garrick said. "My town was attacked by orcs ..." his voice, and his emotions cracked.

"What is your name?" the figure asked. The voice was masculine and deep, echoing through the hall.

"G-Garrick," he answered.

"Garrick. Do you know what your name means?"

Garrick shook his head mutely.

"It means 'one who rules by the spear'. You said your town was attacked. Where are the survivors?"

"I think I'm the only one," he said. His throat was dry and he was nervous. He couldn't see the figure's face, only a shadowy form.

"You are strong. I feel it in the air. It radiates from you. Do you want vengeance upon those who have destroyed your town?"

The question took Garrick by surprise. Did he want

vengeance? He struggled with the answer. To deal out punishment on the orcs who killed his parents, his precious Aela. What would it accomplish? Would he feel any less dead inside? He didn't know the answer. He struggled in silence for a long while. The figure waited patiently.

"No, I do not want revenge." He finally said.

"Hm."

"I want the power to keep it from happening to anyone else."

"I can give you power," the figure said. "And you can use it as you will. There is only one thing I require in exchange."

Garrick tilted his head questioningly.

"When I call upon you, you shall answer. And you shall carry out whatever task I give you."

"What will you ask of me?" Garrick questioned.

"That is not for you to think upon. I offer the power you seek. What is your answer?"

"I will do it," Garrick answered.

"Come, kneel before me."

Garrick did as he was instructed. Even as close as he was, he still could not see the figure's appearance.

"Swear your loyalty to me."

Garrick hesitated for a moment, then said, "I am loyal to you."

"Stretch forth your arm," the figure commanded.

Garrick lifted his right arm.

"No, your left arm."

Garrick switched arms and held his left arm out. The figure grabbed hold of him and an intense cold shot through his arm. He groaned softly and the pain seemed to intensify. The middle of his forearm began to burn, but the rest of his arm remained freezing.

The figure let go of him and the cold diminished, but the burning on his forearm remained. He pulled it back and looked at his skin in the torchlight. A cross, upside down and black as night, marred his flesh. He looked up at the figure questioningly.

"You now bear the Mark."

"What mark is it?" Garrick asked.

"The Mark of Mordum."

"Who is Mordum?"

The torches flickered and went out, leaving Garrick in darkness.

"I am," the figure answered.

The torches flared back to life and the figure was gone.

Garrick wondered if he had made the right decision.

● ∞ ● ∞ ●

"I don't know what to say," Kelvin said quietly, his tone somber.

"You don't have to say anything," Garrick replied. "Just know that not every man is what he seems on the outside."

Kelvin nodded mutely. A long while passed before either of them spoke again. "What happened after you received the Mark?"

Garrick rubbed his hands over his face, stopping briefly to scratch the skin beside his ear. "I left the place. I later learned that it was one of Mordum's abandoned temples. There was more food and water than I could ever consume there, but it was lonely. I stayed for a few days, then traveled west. My hometown was on the fringes of the kingdom, far from the larger towns of Talvaard. I walked for days before ending up on the steps on some nobleman's house.

"He was a good man, though. Took me in and cleaned me up. I told him what happened to my town. He wasn't surprised. Apparently, several other towns on the edge of the kingdom had experienced similar fates. What few survivors came through repeated the same story. He sent word to a friend of his that served as a general under the king at the time. The general took a legion out to investigate. They tracked down some of the orcs and slaughtered them. He also offered to help rebuild the towns that had been destroyed, but the king refused to finance it."

Kelvin shook his head in disbelief.

"I hated him for it. I don't now, but I did then. I guess I had to blame someone for what happened. Although I had the Mark, I didn't know what it did or how to use it. I joined the king's army to learn how to use a blade and one of the generals took an interest in me. He mentored me and taught me everything I know about war." Garrick smiled fondly at the memories.

"Sir," Kelvin said.

"I told you to call me Garrick."

"Sir," Kelvin repeated, his tone more urgent. "Look!"

Garrick turned to where Kelvin was pointing and saw a large formation of elves coming toward them. There were too many to count, but Garrick guessed there were at least a hundred.

"They are moving too fast for us to make a run for it," Garrick said.

"Where would we go? We're surrounded by desert for miles."

"True," Garrick replied. He stood up and brushed the sand from his pants. He looked back to Kelvin. "There's only one option," he said. "We have to fight."

Kelvin stood up and nodded.

They both summoned their armor. The air hissed loudly. Garrick summoned his blade and looked at Kelvin's silver armor, glinting radiantly in the bright sun. He turned his gaze back to the approaching elves.

"Who would have ever thought?" he asked.

"Ever thought what?"

"That a templar of Mordum and a priest of Zevea would ever be fighting together instead of themselves?" he said with a laugh. When he didn't hear Kelvin say anything, he looked over at him just in time to see the pommel of Kelvin's sword coming straight for his face.

The blow struck him hard and he dropped to his knees, the world spinning around him. He wanted to say something, but his mouth didn't work. He looked at Kelvin through watery eyes.

Kelvin's face was impassive, unreadable.

"I'm sorry," he said.

Garrick scrunched his face in confusion. Kelvin struck him again and he fell unconscious into the sand.

Kelvin knelt beside him and tried to ignore the sounds of the elves coming. He closed his eyes, placed his hand on Garrick's chest, and began to pray.

"Nothing I do is in vain if it avenges my father's death."

—Prince Aramis

CHAPTER 13

Aramis walked into the village tiredly and looked for the druid he had spoken with. He saw several people but didn't recognize any of them. Making his way to the center of the village, he saw Kaldrick. The man hadn't noticed him yet. He was talking with one of the druids. He also had a travel sack strapped to his back. As he neared the two men, Kaldrick noticed him.

"My Lord?" he asked, several emotions shadowing his face.

Aramis raised a hand in greeting, too tired to speak.

Kaldrick wrapped him in a strong hug. Aramis didn't try to fight him off. He was too exhausted. Kaldrick released him and looked him over.

"You look rough," he said with a grin.

Aramis looked to the druid. "The creature that caused the plague has been killed," he said.

The druid stood silent for a moment. "I am not one to take pleasure in death, but this news does indeed lift my spirits. How did you kill it?"

Aramis honestly didn't know. Everything was hazy. "I'm not sure," he answered. "I have never seen anything like it before. It seemed to be made up of a few different animals."

The druid's eyes widened. "Can you describe it to me?"

"It had the head of a large cat, the body of a bull and the feet of a bird."

"A chimera," the druid breathed. "You defeated a chimera? Alone?"

Aramis shrugged. "I can't remember what happened," he sighed. "I hate to be rude, but I am in desperate need of some rest."

"Of course," the druid replied. "My apologies. Come with me. You can sleep at my house."

Aramis and Kaldrick followed the druid.

"What's the bag for?" Aramis asked Kaldrick.

"I'm sorry, my Lord. When you didn't return, I feared you were …" he trailed off. "I was getting ready to leave."

Aramis's confusion was evident on his face. "I've only been gone a few hours," he said.

"You've been gone a full week to the day," the druid chimed in.

Aramis's mind reeled in shock. "A week?" How had he been gone that long? It certainly didn't feel like it. Perhaps that was why he was so tired. He followed in silence, digesting the information. The druid led them to his home, the same place Aramis had been to earlier. He allowed Aramis to rest in his bed and left him alone with Kaldrick.

"I am glad to see you, my Lord."

Aramis smiled tiredly and nodded. "I am glad to see you as well. I feared that I would never escape that place." He closed his eyes. The druid's bed was very comfortable.

"What happened?"

When Aramis didn't answer, Kaldrick realized he was asleep. He turned and quietly left the room.

● ∞ ● ∞ ●

He opened his eyes. Confusion overwhelmed him as he didn't recognize anything around him. He had fallen asleep in the druid's home, yet he was lying on a cold stone floor. He sat up and inspected his surroundings. He was either in a castle or a dungeon. The ceiling, walls, and floor were all made of the same smooth stone.

Pushing himself up off the floor, Aramis realized his hands were covered in dirt. He brushed them off on his pants and noticed the entire floor was covered in a thick layer of dust. There were no footprints or anything else indicating anyone had brought him here or that he had made his own way into the room. The outline of where his body lay was the only spot not covered with dust.

Aramis didn't find anything of interest in the room. He left through the only doorway and wandered along the halls. There were no torches or light of any kind, yet he was able to see decently well. He passed by a few rooms that were similar to the one he woke up in. Those rooms, as well as the hallways, also had a layer of dust covering the floors. That gave Aramis the idea that no one had been in the place in a very long time.

The end of the hall split left and right. Aramis paused, not sure which direction he should go first. He started to go right. The tattoo on his arm began to itch. He stopped and changed direction. He followed the hall until it ended. Two large wooden doors stood closed before him. He pushed one and struggled with it for a few moments before it creaked open. He checked the hinges and saw they were rusted from disuse.

He stepped into the room and stared in surprise. Ghostly figures were everywhere. Some sat at long tables looking through papers and writing, others were walking from one table to another, conversing with other people. They were all dressed in the same clothing, white hooded robes with blue sashes around their waists. On the right side of the chest was a symbol stitched into the material: a sun with outstretched wings.

Aramis had never seen it before. At the back of the room stood a man with his hands behind his back. He was dressed the same as the others, but the symbol on his chest was different. It was two swords crossed over each other. He didn't recognize that one either. He wondered what he was seeing. He could see the mouths of the people moving, but he didn't hear any words.

His tattoo was burning strongly. He rubbed at it and walked further into the room. The people reminded him of the priests of Edria, though none of them wore her symbol.

"What are you doing here?"

The voice startled him and he turned to see the man at the back of the room looking at him.

"I don't know," Aramis answered. "What is this place?"

The man ignored the question and continued to stare at him. Aramis walked through the room and came to stand before the man.

"I don't know how I got here. What is this place? Who are you people?"

"You are supposed to be guarding the body."

Aramis frowned. "What?"

Another figure stepped up beside him and Aramis realized the apparition wasn't talking to him, but to the other ghost.

"My apologies, Prophet. I left the body in the hands of capable men until I return. He has yet to move. I believe he is completely immobilized, if not dead."

"Explain to me how the God of the Dead could possibly be dead himself?"

Aramis realized they were talking about Mordum.

"I am not in familiar territory, so I apologize for any presumptions I make."

The Prophet sighed. "No, I must apologize to you. I am weary. This war has exhausted us all, and now that we are close to victory, I am struggling to ensure the safety of the world. It is a heavy burden."

"I can't imagine," the other priest replied. "I take no offense at your words. Have the others found the answer yet?" The priest turned to regard the others working at the tables.

"Not yet," the Prophet answered. "Tael has told me that the answer lies in one of these manuscripts. I fear time is against us, however. The longer it takes to find the answer, the more opportunity Mordum has to break the spell."

Aramis recognized the name Tael, but he couldn't remember where he'd heard it before.

"I understand. I will return to my post. I merely wanted to know how the search was going." The priest left and the room became quiet again. Aramis went over to one of the tables and looked at the papers that littered the surface. They were covered in writing, but he couldn't read the script. He assumed it was another language.

"I think I've found something!" one of the priests shouted. He was sitting at one of the further tables.

"Bring it to me," the Prophet said.

The priest scrambled up from the table and ran to the Prophet, a single parchment in his hand. He handed it to the Prophet. Aramis walked over to them and looked at it over the Prophet's shoulder. Again, he didn't recognize the language that flowed across it, but he did recognize a symbol on it. The black cross of Mordum was penned at the top.

"Is this it? Is this what we've been looking for?" the priest asked.

"I believe it is," the Prophet answered, relief evident in his voice.

A ragged cheer rang out from the other priests in the room.

"What do we need to start with?" the priest asked.

The Prophet's eyes scanned back and forth over the text. "We must burn his body."

"That seems easy enough."

"Not quite. We must burn his body on his own altar using wood from the sacred trees of Tylhem Forest. Then his bones must be separated from the ashes using a Holy Blade. The bones and the ashes need to be kept away from one another."

"We will begin the preparations now. Where should we send his bones?"

The Prophet seemed to consider the question for a long while. "Take the bones to Red Mountain in the Deadlands. We will entrust them to the wizard. As for the ashes ..." Aramis tried to hear the next part, but everything began to fade from his vision.

His eyes opened and he found himself back in the home of the druid.

● ∞ ● ∞ ●

"I know what Mordum's followers want from the Deadlands," Aramis said as he practically ran into the druid. He wasn't sure how long he'd slept, but it didn't seem long. The sun had yet to set and the people were still going about their normal duties.

"I wondered if you would ever wake," the druid replied with a friendly smile.

"What do you mean?" Aramis asked.

"You slept through the remainder of yesterday, all through the night, and most of today."

"I did?" Aramis was shocked. He certainly felt rested, but he didn't feel like he'd spent that much time sleeping.

"You did," the druid confirmed. "But you mentioned something about Mordum?"

"Yes. I had a dream or a vision. I'm not sure which. What I saw, if it was real, explains a few things. What do you know about Mordum?"

The druid shrugged. "As much as anyone else, I suppose. He is the God of the Dead. His followers are very powerful. Or insane. Or both."

"Has he ever walked the earth as a man?"

"Ah," the druid nodded, "you are referring to the Dead Epoch?"

"The what?" Aramis wasn't sure if the druid had asked a question or was stating a fact.

"The Dead Epoch. Historians say it was a dark time for the world. They say Mordum walked the earth in the form of a mortal man. His armies came close to devouring the entire world. The other gods stepped in and gave man what they needed to stop him."

Aramis had never heard that before. He'd heard of the Lord Aio several years ago, but that religion had all but vanished, especially after the Five Islands were destroyed by Orlek. It was said of the Lord Aio that he was a god who came and walked among men as well.

"That seems to match what I saw," Aramis said. "There were men who looked like priests. Two of them had a conversation about Mordum's body. They stopped him somehow, and they were trying to find a way to banish him. They needed to burn the body using wood from your sacred trees."

The druid's face lit up with interest. "That would

explain why he targeted our forest."

"Yes. They separated his bones from his ashes and the bones were sent to the Red Mountain in the Deadlands."

"That's north of here," the druid said. "What about the ashes?"

"I don't know," Aramis lost some of his excitement. "The vision faded before I could hear where they might be."

The druid stroked his goatee. "It's whispered a powerful wizard lives on Red Mountain. I don't know if there is any truth to it or not."

"The men in my vision mentioned a wizard," Aramis said. "How long ago was the Dead Epoch?"

"Hundreds of years," the druid replied, shaking his head. "I don't know the exact amount."

"How could a person, even a wizard, live that long?"

The druid merely shrugged again. "Magic can prolong one's life, but there's no telling how long. Death is inevitable for even the most powerful."

"I need to leave immediately," Aramis said, the excitement coming back into his voice. "Where is Kaldrick?"

"He went to the stream to get some water."

"I appreciate you taking care of him. And thank you for your hospitality. I'm in your debt."

"Nonsense," the druid said. "You killed the creature that brought the plague on our home. Even now I feel its foulness fading. If anything, we are indebted to you. If you ever need anything, call on us."

"I may soon call on you to honor your word."

"Please do. In the meantime, take whatever supplies you need for your journey." They clasped hands and shook, then Aramis turned and left to find Kaldrick. It didn't take long to find him. He was returning from the stream and they met at the wooden bridge.

"It's good to see you alive," Kaldrick said.

"It's good to feel alive," Aramis replied. "We need to leave immediately. We've got to get to Red Mountain before Mordum's followers do."

"I'm waiting on you," Kaldrick laughed.

They filled two packs until they were bursting at the seams with food. The druids gave them fresh bread, fruits, cheese and some strips of venison. Aramis was eager to get moving, so they expressed their thanks to the druids and left just as the sun was setting. They lit torches and walked all through the night. They stopped for a short time in the morning so Kaldrick could take a nap and then they continued on, Aramis leading the way with determination.

He was glad that Kaldrick didn't complain about the pace he set. After all, they had been through, Aramis knew it would probably have done them both some good to rest a few days. Something inside told him to keep moving, though. He didn't know why, but he felt the need to get to Red Mountain as quickly as he could. Perhaps Mordum's followers were on their way there just as he was.

"I have a question," Kaldrick asked as they trekked through the forest.

"Ask away," Aramis replied. He wiped sweat from his brow with the back of his hand. He couldn't understand how the druids lived in the forest, especially not with their thick robes. Aramis felt like he would die from sweating and he wasn't even wearing armor.

"When we were fighting those creatures, I saw you fall. I thought those creatures had killed you. There was blood everywhere. And then … you got up and you had a sword. You don't have a scratch on you. You slaughtered those creatures easily. How? Where are your battle wounds? And where is the sword you had?"

Aramis wasn't surprised by the questions. He had a

few of his own. The problem was he had no one to get answers from.

"I thought I was dying," he began slowly, trying to recollect the details. "I was buried under those creatures and I could feel them ripping my skin off." He shuddered as he remembered the feeling. "It's a little foggy after that. All I remember is I opened my eyes and felt the hilt of a blade in my hand. This," Aramis pointed to the tattoo on his arm, "has connected me to a power that I can't explain. It heals me when I get injured. And it allowed me to … create a sword? I'm not sure how it works."

"So you are like a god?" Kaldrick asked curiously.

"Far from it," Aramis replied acidly. The words came out sounding hateful. "Sorry," he said. "I don't mean to be rude. It's just … it feels like I am nothing more than a pawn on a chess board and some god is controlling my future."

"We may indeed be pawns to higher powers, but that doesn't mean we don't make our own choices. They may be able to influence us, but ultimately we make our own way."

"True," Aramis agreed.

"Can you make the blade appear only when you are in trouble? Or can you make it appear on command?"

"That's a good question," Aramis said. He was curious himself. He stopped walking and focused on the power flowing through his tattoo. He summoned the blade. The air hissed and mist formed around his hand. Within seconds, the blade had fully formed.

"Now that," Kaldrick breathed, "is amazing."

Aramis nodded in agreement. He dismissed the blade and the air hissed as it disappeared. "That's good to know," he said. "I *can* summon and dismiss it on command." He continued walking.

"What about the creature you saw in the portal? How

did you kill it?"

"I don't know. It was massive, bigger than anything I've ever seen."

"Bigger than a phiebus?"

"Much bigger," Aramis said. "I've never felt fear so intensely before. It crushed my neck with one hand." His hands instinctively went to his neck, feeling for any defects that might not have been healed. His skin was flawless. "I can't remember anything after that. When I came to, the creature was dead in a pool of blood. My dagger had some blood on it, but I don't know how I could have killed it. The dagger is old and rusted. It's not even that sharp."

"Maybe your tattoo power helped?"

"Maybe," Aramis said. He was unconvinced. Something wasn't right about that encounter, but he had no idea what.

"I wonder what the desert is like," Kaldrick asked, changing the subject.

"We're about to find out," Aramis answered.

After two days, they reached the end of the forest. Flat grassland stretched out before them. A full day of travel and they began to see patches of sand. They rested for the night and continued on early in the morning. The Deadlands was unlike any place either of them had ever been.

● ∞ ● ∞ ●

Two rough, terrible weeks later they reached what was unmistakably Red Mountain. They had run out of water only a few days into the trek and had quickly learned that it was better to travel at night than during the day. It was much cooler and allowed them to travel faster and farther without the danger of overheating. During one night, they had stumbled upon a small rocky expanse. The smooth flat rocks had water sitting on them. It had been warm and had an odd taste, but they drank it anyway. They had lost two days as they stayed there long enough to recuperate. It took four days from there to finally reach Red Mountain.

"We're here," Kaldrick said, his voice a little coarse. "We finally made it."

"And yet we've only just begun," Aramis said. They gazed up at the mountain top. He could faintly see the outline of a building. "We've got the climb to the top."

The mountain rose up from the desert landscape, tall and almost completely vertical.

"Great," Kaldrick said, heaving a sigh. "Let's get this over with."

Aramis scratched his jaw and eyed the cliffs of the mountain. The stubble growing on his face was starting to irritate him. He'd thought about summoning his blade to shave, but he didn't want to risk cutting his face in the middle of the desert.

"This isn't going to be easy," he remarked. "There doesn't appear to be any handholds."

Kaldrick's response was a muted grunt.

Aramis studied the mountainside, eyeing everything that resembled a crevice in an attempt to determine the best area to scale up. Deciding on his course, he stepped up to the cliff and gripped the stone with his hands. As he was about to lodge his foot into a small fissure, he heard a voice that didn't belong to Kaldrick. He turned to look and was greeted by the sight of a dozen men—all shirtless—with spears leveled at them both.

One of the men, the one who Aramis assumed had first spoken, said something in a language he didn't understand and thrust the spear forward menacingly. Aramis let go of the cliff face and put his hands up nonthreateningly. The man said something else and motioned with his spear toward Kaldrick.

"I don't understand," Aramis said, shrugging his shoulders. He tried to make his facial expression look confused.

The man repeated himself and when Aramis just stood there, one of the other men grabbed him and roughly shoved him over beside Kaldrick. The armed men started talking to one another, pointing at Aramis sporadically. At one point it seemed to get heated between two of the men. One of them finally seemed to yield, and the man who had spoken to Aramis appeared to win the argument. The men proceeded to bind Aramis and Kaldrick's hands behind their backs with strips of leather, then took up positions in front and behind them.

"I wonder who these people are," Aramis whispered to Kaldrick.

One of the men jabbed him painfully in the ribs with the butt end of his spear. Aramis took that as a sign to keep his mouth shut. The men led them around the west side of the mountain to a set of steps carved into the mountainside. Aramis laughed and shook his head. If it weren't for these men, he and Kaldrick would likely have killed themselves trying to climb up the steep cliff.

The steps were jagged and rocky, forcing him to take care where he stepped. The stairs wound steadily up the mountain. In a few places, the rock had broken and most of the stair was missing. Since he was bound and couldn't use his hands, his captors had to assist him. It was obvious the walkway was rarely used. Aramis was certain where they were being taken, but he didn't know why they would take him exactly where he wanted to go.

It took the better part of an hour before they reached the plateau. Aramis was surprised to find the ground was smooth and looked like it had been polished. The ground was the same red color as the rest of the mountain, but there were black flakes scattered amidst the red as well. It reminded him of the snowflakes he had seen once as a child. He wanted to bend down and get a closer look, but he figured one of the men would strike him again.

They halted suddenly. Aramis couldn't see anything past the men. They were taller than he was and they walked shoulder to shoulder. The thought occurred to him that these men might be soldiers. The more he studied their body language, the more he came to realize they were highly disciplined. They wore loose-fitting white pants and black leather boots. Their skin was a dark tan hue, but it seemed natural and not related to being in the sun.

The men parted and stepped to the sides. A figure dressed in white robes approached them. Aramis couldn't tell if it was a man or a woman until the figure spoke. He spoke the same language as the bare-chested men and they conversed for a few moments before the robed man stepped closer to Aramis.

"What are you doing here?" he asked. He spoke without any hint of an accent. "They say you touched the holy mountain."

"My apologies," Aramis answered. "I didn't know it was holy."

The man waved his hand dismissively. "Why are you here?"

"We've come here in search of something."

"What?"

Aramis hesitated. From the vision he had, it seemed as though the priests had sent the bones of Mordum here to be protected. Would they simply allow him to have them? Would they try to kill him for coming to their holy mountain?

"Well?" the man's tone indicated his impatience.

"The bones of Mordum."

The man stiffened. An awkward silence ensued, then the man turned and stalked away. Their guards stayed put but exchanges glances. The robed man disappeared into the massive doorway of a fortress. Aramis hadn't even noticed the building, likely because the soldiers had blocked his view. It was an imposing structure, towering into the sky hundreds of feet.

Its gray stone walls stood in stark contrast to the red landscape of the mountain. The large entryway had two massive wooden doors. One of them was ajar. Aramis noticed thin vertical apertures spaced along the upper section of the walls. He recognized them as arrow slits. He couldn't tell if anyone was manning them.

After a few minutes had passed, he saw the robed man was coming back. Judging by his demeanor, he was more irritated than before. Stopping a few feet away, he motioned at them with his hand.

"Come on, then," he snapped. Then he turned and began walking back toward the fortress.

Aramis and Kaldrick quickly followed after him. They entered through the door and stepped into a spacious and open chamber. A cool breeze tickled Aramis's skin. A dozen braziers, evenly distributed, ran along the walls to his left and right. He passed an empty divan as they continued further into the room. They walked on soft, thick rugs that were so colorful, they reminded him of some rare birds he had seen once. The man took them to an oversized pillow. Two shirtless men—looking rather bored—stood on either side, fanning the person on the pillow with poles that had giant feathers on the ends.

"Wait here," the man instructed them. He knelt beside the pillow and whispered something to the figure. There was a whispered argument.

"Now!" the figure on the pillow shouted. It was a woman.

Aramis's interest grew as the man stood up and shooed the men away. All three of them left the chamber. The woman rose from the pillow, slow and graceful. The first thing Aramis noticed was that she was almost naked. She wore a thin, sheer loincloth of white material which left little to the imagination. Her breasts were uncovered and Aramis had to fight desperately not to stare at them. Stealing a quick glance, he saw they were round and naturally buoyant. Her skin was a bronzed hue and her eyes were a vibrant green. Her hair was long and reached down past her shoulders, so blonde it was almost silver. Her wrists and ankles glinted with silver and gold bands.

"Well," the woman said, her voice smooth as honey. "What brings you to my home?"

Aramis stuttered on his response, finding it hard to focus. Kaldrick cleared his throat next to him. He'd almost forgotten the man was there. He opened his mouth but no words came out. The woman sighed and spoke a word he didn't understand and couldn't remember. A purple robe flittered down from the ceiling and she grabbed it from the air. She slipped it on but didn't tie it shut. Her body wasn't as revealed, but Aramis still found it enticing.

"I-uh," he stammered. Shaking his head slightly, he started again. "I've come here looking for the bones of Mordum."

Her sapphire eyes seemed to pierce his very soul. She studied him intently for a long moment. "Assuming they were here, whatever could you want with them? I'm sure they are nothing more than dust."

"It's a long story," he answered.

"Well, it's a good thing I have nothing but time." She smiled at him. "Take off your clothes. Both of you."

Aramis and Kaldrick exchanged glances.

"Don't be fools," she said with a laugh. "I've got plenty of men around here to satisfy my needs. Your clothes are filthy and I will not allow them to touch anything in here. I'll have them laundered and patched.

I'll have some other clothes brought for you."

The thought of clean clothes was enough to make him strip down. They both stood there naked, feeling awkward. The woman looked them over and made a noise in her throat.

"I think you should both be bathed as well. You look dirtier than your clothes." She snapped her fingers and several attendants rushed into the room. She nodded toward Aramis and Kaldrick and the servants pulled them out of the chamber, down an enormous hall, and into a room with pools built into the floor. Some of the servants were women and they took them to separate pools and washed them with soft sponges.

Aramis tried not to let his thoughts get the better of him, but he ended up being aroused. The servants acted as if they didn't notice and finished washing him. They rinsed him off with buckets of clean, but cold, water. The chill air in the fortress chilled his skin, giving him gooseflesh. The women dried him off and led him into another room where they gave him fresh clothes to wear.

Leading him back out into the main chamber, he saw a table and benches had been set up. Bowls of fruit, bread, and cheese had been set out. Kaldrick joined him, clean and freshly dressed as well.

"Talk about service," Kaldrick whispered with a grin, nudging Aramis in the ribs.

"It's like being back in the palace," he answered.

"Come and sit," the woman said. Aramis was startled to see she was seated at the table. There had been no one there a moment ago. He obeyed, seating himself at the left side of the table. Kaldrick sat at the right.

"Help yourselves," the woman said, motioning to the food.

Kaldrick did just that, stuffing grapes and cheese into his mouth at the same time. Aramis ate more conservatively.

"Who are you?" he asked the woman between bites.

"You can call me Vashah," she answered. "You couldn't possibly pronounce my real name."

"Your real name?"

Vashah smirked at him. "Who do you think I am?"

Aramis shrugged. "I honestly don't know. A druid in the Tylhelm Forest said that a wizard lived here."

"You've been to the forest, have you?" she seemed overly curious.

"Yes," he answered slowly, eyeing her suspiciously.

"I'm surprised they let you, considering the mark you openly wear on your arm."

Aramis subconsciously rubbed the tattoo. "He wasn't very judgmental."

"That's a surprise. Things must have changed in the last few hundred years." Vashah saw the face Aramis made when she said that. "What do you know about wizards?" she asked.

"A little. They have a city in my kingdom where they are free to study."

"Palindrom," Vashah said.

"You've been there?"

"Of course not," she said disdainfully. "They are not wizards. Sure, they may be able to cast magic, but they are not *true* wizards. True wizards are much more powerful and live much longer than normal humans. There aren't many of us left." She said the last part wistfully, almost sad.

"You are not here to discuss such things though, are you? Tell me your story."

Aramis finished chewing a bite of bread, then related the events of the last few months. He told her everything he could remember. The murder of his father, his torture in the dungeon, his rescue and Mel's magical armor. He even told her about the blind woman he'd encountered on the road several times. His trip to the shrine of

Mordum in the mountains was easy to describe. He hadn't forgotten how the dagger the blind woman had given him had saved his life.

Vashah asked a few questions about the shrine. He answered them and then told her about his trek into Talvaard, his meeting with Garrick, and their capture at Mordum's city. He told her of the Prophet's betrayal with hesitation. She listened intently, seeming to devour his every word. He also shared his fragmented memory of his fight with the chimera. She asked more questions about the chimera than anything else.

"That's an interesting tale," Vashah said when he finished.

"You seem surprised by some of it."

"Of course. I don't exactly have the ability to leave this place whenever I want."

"You're a prisoner?" Aramis asked.

"Yes and no. I'm not a prisoner in the sense that someone keeps me locked up in here. I am a prisoner to responsibility." Vashah paused, seeming to consider her words.

"I know the bones are here. I saw them in a vision."

Vashah tilted her head curiously. "A vision?"

Aramis nodded. "I saw a gathering or priests. They were searching for a way to destroy Mordum's body."

The room went quiet except for the sound of Kaldrick eating. Vashah stood and walked to the far end of the chamber. A tall window allowed sunlight in. Aramis rose slowly and joined her at the window. The view was magnificent. The desert stretched out as far as he could see. Here and there he could see the landscape rise and fall in some places.

"I was told by Edria that a messenger would come one day to claim the bones of Mordum. She didn't describe him. She only said I would know him by the mark he carried. I know you bear the mark of Mordum, but I don't understand why Edria would want one of his followers to claim his bones." She turned to face him. Her lips were full and red. Aramis had the overwhelming urged to kiss her. He pushed the thought away.

"I'm not one of his followers," he said. "I was cursed with this mark."

"Have you summoned the armor?" Vashah asked.

"No," he said. She seemed relieved. "I have summoned the blade."

"So you haven't fully accepted the mark. That is good. I have never taken sides with any god, but I've never been able to stomach Mordum or his slaves."

"I'm trying to keep his followers from getting the bones. They already have the blood from the shrine."

"What of the ashes? Have the followers found them?"

"I don't think so," Aramis answered. "I don't know where they are either. The vision ended before I could hear where they sent them."

"A pity," she said. "The priests didn't entrust me with that information." She looked back out the window. "You are more than welcome to have the bones."

Excitement flooded through Aramis. "Really?"

"Yes. There is a catch, however."

"What kind of catch?" His enthusiasm lowered.

"You'll have to retrieve it from the Nexus."

"What is the Nexus?"

"It is a dangerous place designed to protect the bones. Powerful creatures and magic guard them. The pathways around the Nexus are like a maze, each one leading to something different. Only one of the paths lead to the center, the Nexus, where the bones are kept."

"I went into a hellish place and fought a chimera," Aramis said. "Is it worse than that?"

"Much worse," Vashah answered.

"How do you know? Have you been there?"

"No. I designed it."

After they had finished eating, Vashah had her servants take them to different rooms for the night. Aramis had fallen asleep almost immediately. He awoke and was startled when he didn't remember where he was. As his mind slowly became more aware, he remembered the trek through the desert and that they had made it to their destination.

Rolling out of the plush bed, he made his way to the door. As soon as he opened it, he was greeted by servants. They swirled around him, taking off his borrowed clothes and replacing them with his clothes. They were soft and smelled of lavender. The holes had been patched with such skill, he almost couldn't tell where they had been. The servants led him to the main chamber. Vashah and Kaldrick were already at the table eating breakfast. Aramis sat down with them and grabbed an apple from one of the bowls.

"Where does all this food come from?" he asked.

Vashah smiled at him. "What sort of wizard would I be if I couldn't conjure up anything I want?"

Aramis shrugged. He didn't know much about magic.

"As soon as you are ready, I will take you to the Nexus. Your friend will have to stay with me."

"What do you mean? Why can't he go with me?"

"Only someone who bears the mark of Mordum can enter," Vashah answered.

"If you are trying to protect the bones from being taken by one of his followers, why would you only allow someone with his mark to enter? Doesn't that defeat the purpose?"

"The Nexus is designed to be a death trap," Vashah said with a laugh.

Suddenly Aramis wasn't so sure about everything. He'd seen the power of Mordum's templars and didn't have any doubts that they could defeat anything thrown at them. They had powers given to them by a god. What could a wizard conjure to stop the power of a god? Aramis could summon a blade, but he was nothing compared to a templar. He didn't know if he had the strength to complete this task. He realized Vashah and Kaldrick were staring at him.

"Are you sure about this?" Kaldrick asked worriedly.

"No," Aramis said, "but if I don't get them, it's likely Mordum's followers will get them. And we can't let that happen."

"Everything in the Nexus is deadly, but there are two creatures especially that you should be wary of," Vashah said. "The Lamia and the Jackalwere."

"What are those?" Kaldrick asked.

"The Lamia are half snake, half human creatures. Their upper body is the human part, and the rest is a snake. They are quick and clever. If you see one, run the other way. A Jackalwere is a doglike creature that walks on two legs. Their claws are wickedly sharp and their teeth contain venom that can paralyze you within seconds. Both of these creatures are drawn to the power that flows through the tattoo."

Kaldrick looked at Aramis, the concern evident on his face. Aramis digested the information, trying not to let it worry him. He wasn't afraid of the fact that he had to go in alone. No, that did not worry him. He'd gone into the shrine by himself to get the blood. This was different because he was afraid of failing. If he failed, his kingdom would remain in the hands of the usurper. Only the gods knew if they'd be taken care of. His father's killer would go unpunished. Mordum would take on human flesh and bring war across the world.

Aramis steeled his nerves and forced his mind to control his emotions. Failure was *not* an option. He smiled at Kaldrick to calm him down.

"I'll be fine," he added.

Kaldrick looked doubtful for a moment, then nodded. He didn't say anything further as they continued their breakfast. Aramis knew he needed to eat so he'd have enough energy to do whatever he needed to survive, but he wasn't really hungry. He finished off the apple and picked apart a bread roll, not really eating much of it. Convincing himself he was ready, he stood up.

Vashah snapped her fingers and her servants came running. They cleared the table off with quiet, quick efficiency. Aramis admired their hard work. *If only the servants in the castle were half as skilled*, he thought.

"Follow me," Vashah said. She led them out of the main chamber and down the hallway where their rooms were. They continued to the end of the corridor, then turned left. They went down a massive spiral staircase carved of the same stone as the rest of the fortress. When they reached the bottom, torches suddenly burst into life, lighting up a small room with a single door. It was plain and unadorned.

"This is the door to the Nexus," Vashah announced. "I'll need to shut the door quickly to ensure nothing escapes. As soon as you are ready, I will open it for you."

Aramis inhaled deeply, preparing himself mentally. He tilted his neck to the left until it cracked, then repeated the motion for the other side. He walked over to the door and held his hand out, summoning his blade. The air hissed as it formed in his grasp. He looked to Vashah and nodded.

The wizard closed her eyes and began chanting softly. Runes on the door began to glow with a soft white light. The ground began to tremble slightly as the door began to open. When it had opened a quarter of the way, Vashah opened her eyes.

"Go now!"

Aramis sprinted through the opening and was

plunged into darkness.

"The gods wage war but it is their followers who die."

—General Garrick

CHAPTER 14

Adamar sat at his desk reading through financial ledgers when a knock interrupted him. He looked up from the mass of numbers and nodded toward one of his guards. The robed templar moved noiselessly to the door and opened it. A sweaty and breathless messenger stood in the doorway.

"Enter," Adamar said as he went back to studying the numbers.

The messenger walked in and kneeled down beside the desk.

"Rise," Adamar said with an air of boredom. He was focused on the ledgers. Something about the numbers from the tax collectors wasn't right, but he couldn't find the error. He went line by line, tallying the numbers with an abacus. He eyed the page and began to get irritated.

The messenger rose to his feet. He waited for the king to look at him. When he didn't, the man glanced to the templar. Receiving no sign from him either, the man decided to deliver the message.

"King Adamar, I have news regarding the bones of

Mordum.”

Adamar turned his full attention on the messenger. The intensity of his gaze caused the man to stumble over his words.

“Speak!” Adamar commanded angrily. The messenger took a deep breath.

“Your spies have located the bones of Mordum.”

“Where?”

“The Deadlands. Far to the north at a place called Red Mountain.”

“The Deadlands?” Adamar stood and walked over to a large table at the back of the room. Spread out on the surface were maps of every size and shape. He eyed the distance and began estimating the time it would take to get troops there.

“I have a battalion that can make the trip in six days. Seven including the time it takes to dispatch orders to them.”

“There’s something else, my Lord.”

“Yes?” he asked, still staring at the maps.

“The spies also indicate your brother has made an appearance.”

“Where?”

“He’s at Red Mountain as we speak.”

“What?” Adamar spun around swiftly. “What is he doing there?”

The messenger shrugged. “That was not in the report.”

Adamar turned back to the maps and slammed his fist down onto the table. “Call for my generals!” he yelled.

“My Lord,” the messenger continued, “the report was delivered today, but the general who received it initially from the spies has already ordered his men to march on Red Mountain.”

“That’s a bit of excellent news,” Adamar said, the news calming him somewhat. “When will they arrive?”

"According to the general, they should arrive at the mountain today. Tomorrow at the latest."

Adamar took in the information. The man responsible needed a promotion. "Is there anything else?"

"No, sir."

Adamar walked back to his desk and sat down. A servant poured him a glass of wine, which he downed in a long drink. He looked back at the ledger and immediately found the error. He looked to the messenger who was still standing there, waiting to be dismissed.

"How many shops are in the market?" he asked.

The messenger's face contorted in thought. "I believe there are one hundred shops."

"Exactly one hundred?"

"Yes, my Lord."

"Thank you. You can go."

The messenger left the room. Adamar looked to the templar who had opened the door. "Find the bookkeeper for the market district. He's been stealing from me," he said. The templar bowed and headed for the door.

"I want you to kill him," he added as an afterthought. "And bring me his skull."

The templar tilted his head in acknowledgment.

Now that he'd found the error, he adjusted the totals. Satisfied everything matched up correctly, he signed the ledger and closed the book. The servant who poured his wine refilled the glass and collected the stack of ledgers on the desk and carried them off.

Adamar was close to having the bones of Mordum and yet somehow his blasted brother was one step ahead of him. He should have killed the brat when his mother was pregnant. Adamar drummed his fingers on his desk, contemplating what he would do if his men failed to secure the bones. There were three items he needed to bring his dark god into a fleshly body, and he didn't have any of them.

At least I know where two of them are, he mused. *It could be worse.*

They were the key to securing his Mark. He wanted the Mark more than anything he'd ever desired. He needed it. Desperately. He drank the wine and pushed the thought from his mind. Standing up, he left the private study that was attached to his bedchamber. Servants quickly gathered around him and pulled his clothes off, replacing them with armor. It was made of gold and silver, more for ceremony than for actual use. They worked quickly and efficiently, using oiled cloths to remove any smudges.

Adamar admired his own appearance in a tall mirror once they had finished. The armor glinted like a stunning jewel. The majority of the breastplate was silver. Etched into the metal were large decorative symbols in gold, and the edges of his bracers and greaves were trimmed in gold as well. He turned and left the room, his remaining templar bodyguard falling into step behind him.

He was going out to the barracks to see his troops and ensure their loyalty to his cause. Initially, he'd lost a large number of soldiers. They were loyal to his brother, so he didn't mourn their departure. There were a few dissenters who stayed and tried to cause trouble. They loudly voiced their opinions and spread rumors like wildfire. Adamar had them flogged. When they continued with their opposition, he had them killed.

For the most part, the nobles had welcomed him with open arms. He had received lavish gifts from all of them. He knew it was a show. If anyone else had taken the throne, they would have done the same thing. He didn't let it bother him. The nobles were dependent upon the king for their land and their status. Likewise, he was dependent upon them for their support and the taxes they paid. Were they to band together and rise against him ...

he pushed the thought away. They were not the warriors they thought they were. Besides, he controlled the kingdom's military. If they did rise up, he would quickly crush their rebellion.

Adamar exited the castle and made his way to the barracks. The barracks consisted of six large buildings, all within the castle's protective walls. They were square in design with two stories. The first floor had a kitchen and a massive dining area where the men ate in shifts. The second floor, accessible from within the building as well as without, housed the rooms where the men slept. Each building could comfortably house five thousand men, seven thousand if comfort wasn't an option. Unfortunately, two of the buildings sat empty, the result of the recent departure of soldiers loyal to Aramis.

A messenger met him halfway to the first building, waving his arms wildly. His shirt was a little too big for him and his sleeves rippled as he waved, reminding Adamar of flags blowing in the wind.

"My Lord," he called out shrilly. "My Lord! The generals asked me to inform you of their location. They've gathered outside the walls for training drills. They've asked that you meet them there."

Adamar stopped mid-stride, turned, and headed toward the castle gate. He hoped this wasn't some attempt to irritate him. He didn't like changes without proper notifications. His bodyguard followed along quietly.

Leaving the castle behind, he made his way to the fields where the soldiers were training. The sight of twenty thousand men in military formation was stunning. As a boy, he'd always wanted to ride at the head of an army, leading his troops into battle. Now that he was king, he would get his opportunity. As soon as he had the favor of the common people, he would lead his army in Oakvalor and expand his kingdom.

"My Lord," one of the generals greeted as Adamar approached. "My apologies for not sending word earlier. This was a last minute decision."

"Understandable," Adamar replied. "Don't let it happen again."

"This was a one-time mistake," the general said.

"Show me what you are doing out here."

The general motioned to his peers. They began issuing commands to young men, who in turn relayed the messages to men holding large flags. Those men, called flag bearers, then began waving the flags in specific patterns.

"Those patterns were used to inform the soldiers what they should be doing," the man said. "It's much quicker than sending runners into the field."

"How so?" Adamar asked.

"Once fighting commences, there isn't much order. You're as likely to strike a friend as you are an enemy. The runners can get killed or turned around and unable to find the captains. So instead we use these flag patterns to send messages."

"Does it work?"

"Well …" the general paused. "We don't know yet. We've not used it in an actual battle, but in these training sessions it works very well."

Adamar nodded and watched as the formations split and changed directions as the flags waved. "I like it," he said. "Whose idea was this?"

The general cleared his throat. "Prince Aramis's."

"I see." Adamar frowned. As much as he wanted his brother dead, he had to admit that the idea was clever. "A good idea is good whether it comes from a fool or a wise man. Continue using the patterns. I want this system perfected in the next six months."

"Yes, my Lord. A question, if I may?"

Adamar nodded.

"What's in six months?"

Adamar smiled. "The expansion of my kingdom."

He turned and walked away, leaving the general to figure out his words alone. Adamar returned to the castle and retired to his personal chamber. The armor was beautiful but stifling. It was a good thing it was only for show. He'd never be able to fight in it for all the sweating.

He sat down on a pillowed chair and relaxed, flipping through a book he'd found in his father's wardrobe. Most of it didn't make any sense, just scribbled drawings and half-written sentences. A servant brought him some wine and fruit to tide him over until dinner was prepared. He must have dozed off, for he startled awake when his head began slipping sideways.

He cleared his throat and looked around the room. It was empty except for his lone bodyguard. He wondered where the other one was. He should have killed the bookkeeper and returned with his head already. Maybe he'd gotten lost in the market.

Adamar was about to close the book he'd been looking through when something caught his attention. He rubbed the sleep from his eyes and lifted the book up closer to his face. The half sentences that caught his attention said:

Deep below lies a secret ...
Sent long ago to keep it ...
Black and gray and sifted ...
Behind red stones shifted ...

Adamar read the words again several times. His heart began to beat excitedly in his chest. These words were referencing the ashes of Mordum. The third key to bringing the dark god into a mortal body.

"Yes!" he shouted aloud.

The templar looked at him.

"The ashes of Mordum. I know where they are!"

The templar gave him a questioning look. Adamar found the man's lack of speech irritating. "They are here," he said.

The templar looked around the room.

"Not *here*. Here," Adamar waved his hand, encompassing the castle. "When I was a child, I saw a room deep in the dungeon. I used to hide there and make the servants find me. One of the walls had red stones in it. I don't remember the design, but I remember the color. It reminded me of blood."

The door to the chamber opened suddenly and the other templar walked in.

"It's about time," Adamar snapped. "What took you so long? Nevermind that," he said, shaking his head, "we need to get down to the dungeon." Adamar noticed the templar was carrying a severed head.

"When I said bring me his skull, I didn't mean bring it to my bed—" the words died on his lips. The severed head wasn't the bookkeeper's. It was the templar's. Adamar's eyes widened in surprise.

The other templar had already noticed. The guard had summoned his armor and blade and was rushing toward the imposter. Adamar quickly scrambled to the edge of the room, moving to stand in front of the window.

Tossing the head aside, the imposter removed the templar's robes to reveal an older man in silver armor. Adamar immediately recognized the insignia on the breastplate as the symbol of Edria—a closed hand with an open eye in the center. How had the priest killed his guard? Mordum's knights controlled fearsome powers.

"Kill him!" Adamar screamed in fury.

The priest of Edria lifted his hand and summoned his blade. A blinding light filled the room and a thunderous *boom* shook the floor. Adamar's fury quickly changed to fear. Armor and blades from the gods hissed when summoned. The only difference was …

"The Prophet," Adamar whispered. Only a Prophet's blade created such a spectacle. He'd never seen one, but he'd heard stories of Mordum's Prophet summoning his. Flashes of black lightning and blue flames.

"I've come for a reckoning!" the Prophet of Edria shouted. "Your dark god may have killed my precious Edria, but I will make the tally even!"

The templar and the prophet collided in a clash of blades. Adamar stood transfixed, watching the battle unfold before him. He didn't know what he should do. The templar would kill the prophet. Wouldn't he? Adamar looked to the discarded head and had his doubts. He turned to the window and pushed on it. The glass pane pushed outward easily. Adamar looked down. He was hundreds of feet above the ground. He looked back at the battle. They seemed fairly matched. Hopefully, he wouldn't have to jump. He'd never survive, but it was better than dying at the hands of the Prophet.

Soldiers appeared in the doorway and attempted to apprehend the Prophet. He cut them down without a backward glance. He appeared to have the advantage as he was driving the templar back. Adamar climbed onto the ledge. His hands were sweating profusely and his legs were involuntarily shuddering. He flexed his leg muscles, trying to regain control of them.

More soldiers spilled into the room. Suddenly the Prophet inhaled sharply. Adamar struggled to see what was happening. The templar's blade was covered with blood. The Prophet staggered back, clutching his stomach. Turning his hate-filled eyes on Adamar, the Prophet lifted his blade and spoke a word. A blinding light filled the room and then the man was gone.

Adamar jumped down from the ledge and was quickly surrounded by soldiers. The templar was covered with sweat and blood, but none of the blood appeared to be his own.

"You almost killed him," Adamar said. "You defended my life."

The templar merely bowed his head in reply.

"How did he get inside my castle?" he asked aloud. "Double the guard. No, triple it! I want every soldier on duty!" The soldiers scrambled out of the room to comply. Once they were gone, servants came in and began cleaning up the mess from the fight.

Adamar slumped into the pillowed chair. This was exactly why he needed the Mark. What if the Prophet had managed to kill both of his templars? He could have been killed. He slammed a fist on the arm of the chair in frustration and anger.

"How dare Edria's followers come here and try to kill me!" he shouted. He ordered one of the servants to bring him some wine. After he'd consumed a few glasses, his nerves had calmed. He sent a messenger to retrieve one of his generals. Half an hour later, the general appeared in the doorway.

"Gather some workers," Adamar commanded. "I need them in the dungeon for a project. Bring some of your men, too. No one sleeps until this project is done."

The general bowed and left.

● ∞ ● ∞ ●

It was in the early hours of the next morning when the workers managed to remove the red stones from the wall. Looking at it now, Adamar realized that the stones had been arranged in the symbol of Mordum. Once the workers cleared the way, he ordered them out of the room. Then he ordered the soldiers to kill them.

"I don't want anyone knowing about this," he explained to the general.

Adamar grabbed a torch from a sconce and stood in front of the demolished wall. He held the torch out in front of him, expecting to see something magnificent holding Mordum's ashes. Instead, he found a long hall that stretched into darkness.

"Grab some torches," he ordered the soldiers. "We're going in."

"Something is coming. I feel it in my bones."

—Prince Aramis

CHAPTER 15

The door slammed shut behind him with a thunderous crash. Aramis stood frozen in place, expecting an army of creatures to suddenly attack him. After what seemed like an eternity, he slowly let his guard down. As his eyes adjusted to the gloom, he realized that he was not in complete darkness as he had first thought.

The ceiling glowed with a faint light. It provided just enough illumination to see by. Aramis looked around and noticed that the walls and floor were crafted from dull bronze colored stones, all interconnected to one another. He estimated the distance between the walls to be about six feet—plenty of room to defend himself.

Keeping a tight grip on the hilt of his sword, he cautiously began to walk forward. He stopped immediately when he felt the stone under his foot shift beneath his weight. Inches ahead, arrows flew forth from holes in the walls. The bolts struck the stones with such force that they lodged tightly in place. Aramis stood in shocked surprise. He knew Vashah said that the place was designed to kill, but he hadn't expected anything dangerous in the entrance.

He decided to take Vashah's warning more seriously. He began testing every stone he stepped on, pressing his weight on them and leaning back to avoid being struck by anything that might come from the walls. It was impossible to judge the passing of time, but he felt like it was taking too long to make any real progress. Concluding he was being too cautious, he picked up the pace and only tested the stones every tenth step.

When he finally reached the end of the hallway, he came to a forked path. There were three hallways before him: left, right, and one straight ahead that appeared to descend. He looked down each hall, trying to decide which way to go. Vashah said the place was a maze. If he went the wrong way, there was no telling how long it would take him to backtrack and get back to where he was now. *If* he could make it back.

He recalled an old saying:

The left-handed path is for the wicked.

Aramis chose the hall to the right.

In the distance, he could hear what sounded like howling. Trying to step as lightly as he could, he followed the hall for a long while. It twisted and turned, but he did not encounter any side passages. Eventually, the hall widened and connected to a large room. Aramis paused at the edge of the hall, testing the stones by pressing his blade on them and applying pressure.

Satisfied there were no traps, he stepped into the room. It was oval in shape and had two doorways, one to the left and one straight ahead. He decided to continue going straight when he saw something move at the edge of his vision. He froze immediately. He turned his head slowly to see what had moved. A rat, a very large rat, skittered along the edge of the wall.

Exhaling the breath he didn't realize he was holding,

Aramis took a step just as a larger shape on four legs entered the room from the doorway to the left and snapped the rat up in its mouth. He heard the sickening sound of bones crunching. The larger shape finished off the rat and lifted its nose into the air, sniffing. Aramis started moving slowly.

The shape stood up on two legs and Aramis saw the glint of red eyes. It was covered in dark brown hair and had two ears standing straight up on the top of its head. Its outline was similar to a man's, but its face was elongated. Torn, dirty bandages were wrapped around its forearms and calves. A tattered material served as pants. It lifted its head and howled loudly.

Aramis sprinted for the doorway and heard the creature take up the chase behind him. The howl was likely a call to its fellows. He needed to find a defensible position, and quickly. He dared not look over his shoulder but he could hear the creature right behind him. Suddenly he threw himself to the ground. The creature tripped over him and landed on the ground in front of him, snarling.

Aramis got back on his feet and ran his blade through the creature's back. A pitiful whelp filled the air, reminding him of a dog. He twisted the blade and jerked it out roughly. Blood pooled around the creature as it struggled weakly to move. Howling echoed off the walls from the room behind him. He ran down the hall, all regard for safety lost.

He felt a stone shift under his foot and grunted as something struck him in the ribs. Gritting his teeth against the pain, he kept running. He could feel something warm and wet running down his skin. *Blood,* he thought. The hall started to become narrow. It was hardly noticeable at first, but as he went further it became obvious. He felt like the walls were steadily coming closer, threatening to crush him.

Finally, he stopped. The space was too narrow. He measured the gap with his hand. From the tips of his fingers to the end of his palm, where his wrist was. He shook his head. It would be too close, especially if it narrowed anymore. He considered going back until he heard the sound of the creatures. He wasn't sure, but it sounded like they were coming closer.

Cursing his luck, he dismissed his blade and forced his body into the narrow gap. He had to suck his stomach in and turn his head sideways. He started to get scared when he felt like he was stuck.

I don't want to die like this.

A sudden howl startled him. The creature was right behind him. More howls followed. He realized there was more than one. Many more. He tried to suck in his stomach even more, but there was nowhere else for his body to squish. He felt something touch his arm and involuntarily gasped.

The creature went wild. It started scrabbling at the narrow gap, trying to reach him. Aramis felt the creature's claws rake his arm. Pain lanced up his shoulder. He pushed himself into the gap further, trying to put more distance between himself and the creature. He recalled Vashah's description of a Jackalwere and assumed that's what he was facing.

It was relentless. He could hear the others growling and snarling. He started to panic when he couldn't move any further. The walls were crushing him. He could only take small breaths. Blood flowed openly from his ribs and his arm. His vision began fading. Aramis stopped fighting and gave himself to the darkness.

● ∞ ● ∞ ●

Aramis looked at his reflection in a large pool of crystal clear water. His hair was a dark gray. His face had many wrinkles, some of them tugging at his eyes. He looked exhausted. The sound of someone approaching grabbed his attention and he turned to see who it was.

A woman who reminded him of an older Hannah smiled at him as she flipped through the pages of a book. She stood a few feet from him and was wearing a beautiful dress. Pearls and other beads of semi-precious stones created a dazzling pattern across the front of the bodice.

"Who are you?" he asked.

The woman laughed playfully. "I'm your wife, silly. Even after all these years, you can still make me smile with such little effort."

Aramis stared at her, confused. He looked around and noticed they were in a garden. Carefully sculpted shrubs in the shapes of mythical animals dotted the cobblestone walkway that surrounded the pool. The pool was perfectly square and had a large statue of a knight in the center. The knight was holding his sword up high, saluting some unseen deity. Water sprayed elegantly from the pommel of the blade, creating a rainbow among the drops of water as they fell.

Looking up, he saw the spires of a massive castle reaching high into the sky. The garden seemed to be located somewhere in the center of the castle around him.

"Where am I?" he asked.

Again, the woman laughed. "Are you okay?" she asked. "You look tired. Perhaps you should retire for the afternoon? I'm sure your son can handle the courtly duties while you rest." She closed the book. The cover looked familiar to him.

"My son?" he asked.

As if following some cue, a young man entered the garden from a doorway in the castle wall and approached them.

"Father," the man greeted.

Aramis stared at him. He was handsome, with short cropped brown hair. His eyes were a dark green and his skin was a bronzed color. His clothes were made of expensive materials. Aramis also recognized they were the colors of the kingdom; Oakvalor's colors of royalty.

"How old am I?" he asked curiously.

The woman and the young man exchanged glances.

"Father," the man said quietly. "Are you well? Should I call the physicians?"

"My love," the woman said, "I'm worried about you. Are you ill?"

Aramis shook his head. "No, I'm fine." He saw the concerned look in their eyes. "I'm just jesting with you." He smiled to make it convincing.

The young man seemed satisfied, but the woman continued to stare at him worriedly.

"Well if you don't need me, I'm going on a hunt with the nobles," the man said. "Lord Bavol insists that I go with them."

"Lord Bavol? He's still alive?" Aramis asked in surprise.

The young man laughed. "Everyone says that. He claims he's the oldest man in Oakvalor, but he also claims he's seen a golden phiebus." The man shook his head, chuckling.

"Have you seen your sister?" the woman asked.

"Not in the past hour. I saw her at breakfast, though. She said something about going to the barracks."

"I wish you'd put a stop to this," the woman said indignantly.

"She doesn't listen to me," the man returned. "You know that."

"I'm talking to your father," the woman said.

Aramis looked from the man to the woman. He was

married and had two children? What was happening?

"What is she doing at the barracks?" he asked.

The woman threw her hands up. "It's as if you aren't aware of anything today," she said exasperatedly. "Your daughter goes to the barracks every day and trains with the soldiers. It's not proper for a woman. Especially not for a princess."

Aramis looked to the man for an explanation, but the man only smiled.

"I'll leave you two to discuss that," he said with a laugh, then turned and walked away.

Aramis turned back to the pool and stared at his reflection again. He looked as old as his father was when he was killed.

"All I'm asking is that you to talk to her," the woman said. She was beside him now.

Aramis turned to her. Only she wasn't there. The beautiful garden was gone too, replaced by a dead landscape. He looked into the pool. It was empty. The castle walls had vanished. The only thing the same was the pool.

"Which of these do you prefer?" a voice behind him asked.

He turned around to see a robed figure, a hood pulled low over his face.

"What's happening?" Aramis asked.

The figure motioned to their surroundings. "This is the future. One of many that could be."

Aramis stared hard at the figure. His skin began to crawl and the terrible smell of death filled his nostrils. "Mordum."

The dark god tilted his head in acknowledgment. "This is the future if you fight my will. The glimpse you saw of your wife is what the future holds if you bow to my will."

"I'll never bow to you," Aramis said, spitting at the

figure.

"You will bow," Mordum answered. "Whether willingly or by force."

Aramis stepped toward the god threateningly, then dropped to his knees in agony. He clutched at his arm where the Mark was.

"Who are you to defy a god?" Mordum asked harshly. "You are nothing. Your life is nothing compared to the eternity I have lived. This world will burn."

"Men stopped you before," Aramis gasped through the pain.

Mordum ignored the comment. "You will obey me." He pointed at Aramis and the skin around his tattoo burned hotter. Aramis collapsed onto the ground, rocking back and forth. And then Mordum was gone. After a few minutes, the pain subsided.

Aramis lay there cradling his arm. He looked at his skin, expecting to see it burned. It wasn't. But the veins in his arm were black. He felt sick. He also felt as though a fire were burning under his flesh. The dark power of Mordum flowed through him, filling his mind with twisted thoughts. He was going mad.

And then he remembered something. The book the woman had been holding. He knew why it was familiar. It was his father's.

● ∞ ● ∞ ●

His eyes fluttered open. To his great displeasure, he was still stuck. He gingerly touched his side with his injured arm. The bleeding had stopped and the wound was closed. That was a small relief. Judging by the dried blood on his arm, he assumed it had healed as well.

Aramis could hear the Jackalwere still scratching at the walls behind him. It wasn't as frantic as before. He tried to push himself forward and failed. The creature's interest was captured again and it tried harder to reach him.

He played through his vision. Why was Mordum so bent on having his loyalty? He didn't know. A disturbing thought entered his mind then. If he summoned his blade, he could cut some of his flesh off to get through the narrow space.

The thought almost made him gag. Was the Mark going to drive him mad? He remembered Mel telling him that while some of Mordum's followers received power, many of them went insane. As he considered the thought, it started to become more appealing. He was stuck. Behind him was a room full of creatures bent on killing him. He didn't know what was ahead, but it had to be better than the alternative.

He summoned the blade with his right hand and the air hissed as it formed. Aramis twisted the blade around until the tip of the blade was pointed toward him. Closing his eyes, he placed the blade against his stomach.

One, two, three ...

He pushed the blade hard and felt the metal bite into his flesh. Agonizing pain assaulted his body. He screamed aloud. He vaguely heard the creature's behind him howling. His body began trembling uncontrollably. He managed to press the sword in a downward motion, cutting the front of his stomach off. He felt blood pouring down the front of his body. So much blood!

Removing the chunk of flesh allowed him to push through the narrow space. Not far ahead, he could make out an opening. He dismissed the blade and slipped forward along the wall. The pain was so intense he thought he might pass out again, but he could also feel the healing power of the Mark kicking in.

A little further ...

Aramis slipped through the opening and fell onto the ground. He was covered in blood. Pulling his torn shirt up, he saw with horror the gaping wound. He could feel vomit trying to rise up his throat. He swallowed hard, trying to keep it down. After several unbearable minutes, the Mark had healed him. His skin had completely grown back. He desperately wanted to sleep. His mind and his body were beyond exhausted.

"I can't," he whispered to himself. "I have to get—"

A sound to his left made him pause. He turned his head slowly. A Jackalwere lay curled up asleep a few feet away. He sat up slowly and quietly and his heart almost stopped at what he saw. The room he was in was full of sleeping Jackalwere. He silently cursed the gods. He looked for an exit and found three. None of them were as close as he would have liked, but at least there was a way out.

He moved as quietly as he could, pausing when his clothes or his boots made noise. He was roughly twenty feet from the nearest doorway but it felt like an eternity away. He heard one of the creatures make a snorting noise. He stepped around their sleeping forms, carefully checking to ensure he didn't step on their hair. From the corner of his vision, he saw the glint of red eyes and froze mid-step. It was smaller than the others and watched him curiously, huddled behind two other still forms.

These things are breeding in here?

Aramis stood still, waiting to see what the creature was going to do. When it didn't move or make a sound, he thought it might be sleeping with its eyes open. He placed his foot on the ground, not watching where he stepped and heard the yelp of a creature. The room became a flurry of motion as the Jackalwere scrambled up to see what the commotion was.

Aramis summoned his blade and removed the head of

the creature he stepped on. He managed to kill two more before the creatures realized what was happening. He was quickly surrounded. They lunged at him, trying to cut him with their wickedly sharp claws. He managed to cut some of their paws off, but there were too many. He was struck several times and they backed him up against a wall. Claws raked across his flesh from all directions and he was quickly covered in gashes and scratches.

He fought to ignore the burning their claws left behind. He knew there was no escape this time. There was no hope. He swung his sword in a wide arc, driving the Jackalwere back momentarily. One of them came at him as his sword passed and he lifted his left arm up to block the creature's swipe. As he did, he noticed that his arm was covered with black lines. The Mark was burning fiercely. He could feel the dark power welling up inside him.

Aramis closed his eyes and let the power flow freely. He was immediately energized. Mist started swirling around him and the creatures drew back in confusion. Aramis was confused as well, but he used the distraction to cut down several more of the Jackalwere.

The air hissed and he felt something closing around his body. He looked down and saw black armor forming around his body. The creatures, having overcome their confusion, came at him with fury. The armor felt weightless and he was able to maneuver as easily as if he weren't wearing any. He reached up and pulled the visor of his helm down. It limited his vision a little, but it protected his face from their claws.

Even though he knew the Mark continuously healed his wounds, he didn't know if it had a limit to its power. If he lost an eye, would the Mark be able to replace it? If he was stabbed in the heart, would it keep him from dying? He allowed his mind to wander as he hacked and slashed his way through the creatures, making his way toward the closest doorway.

One of the creatures began howling, its tone different than the previous howls he had heard. The others took notice too, as they began to start acting nervous. Their heads shifted around and they sniffed at the air. He killed a few more as they began moving in different directions, abandoning the fight. Aramis didn't question his luck and ran toward the exit.

He stopped quickly as soon as he saw the reason for the Jackalwere's reactions. A large snake slithered into the room. It was the size of a horse. Aramis realized it wasn't actually a snake. At least, not all of it. The upper part of the slithering creature was humanoid. It looked like a woman, with long blonde hair. Its skin was pale and had its breasts exposed. From the stomach down it was covered in scales. Its tail swayed back and forth behind it.

Aramis brought his sword up and blocked its tail as it came flying straight at him. The force made him stagger backward. Several of the Jackalwere rushed the snake-human, scratching at it with their claws. He remembered Vashah mentioning this creature as well. A Lamia, she had called it. He watched as the Lamia used its tail to smack the Jackalwere away. One of the creatures slammed into the wall and fell to the ground, unmoving.

He looked toward the other two doorways. Most of the Jackalwere had fled through them, but he didn't see any other option. He sprinted across the room. Quicker than he would ever have imagined, the Lamia shot across the room and intercepted him, slamming its thick, powerful tail against his shoulder. The blow sent him spinning in circles and he crashed to the ground, his armor clattering loudly.

Using his sword, he pushed himself onto his feet and turned to face the creature. In the doorway, he saw three more of the snake-humans slither into the room, crushing and flinging Jackalwere as they entered. The one in front of him whipped its tail around his legs and spun him about, wrapping its thick tail around his entire body. He dropped his sword as the Lamia squeezed him tightly, crushing the air from his lungs. His vision exploded with stars and he thought he could feel his ribs cracking. He was vaguely aware of more snake-humans entering the room.

Just as he thought his chest was going to collapse, a blinding light filled the room. The Lamia used its human hands to cover its eyes, shrieking in a piercing tone. The light was intense, illuminating every corner of the chamber. Aramis felt its grip on him loosen slightly. He sucked in a deep breath and closed his eyes against the light. It blinded him still.

A burning smell filled the air and he gagged as he recognized the scent of burning flesh. He fell backward unexpectedly, landing in something soft. He tried to open his eyes, but the intense light made them water. He blinked several times to clear them but it was no use. And then everything went silent. He wasn't sure, but it seemed like the light began to dim. He heard the sound of footsteps coming toward him. He quickly wiped the tears from his eyes. His vision was still blurred, but he saw the outline of someone standing over him.

As his vision cleared, the features of the figure—a man—started to become visible. The man was wearing silver armor. A symbol was etched into the breastplate: a burning sun with outstretched wings. He'd never seen it before. When he looked upon the man's face, his heart skipped a beat. He stared in shock, unable to speak. There was no mistaking it. His voice failed him several times before he was finally able to speak.

"Mel?"

"If one has power … use it."

—Jovanna

CHAPTER 16

Jovanna found the castle's library to be larger than she expected, especially for a place on the edge of civilization. Tall bookcases lined the chamber, creating aisles that reached from one side of the room to the other.

Jovanna stopped at one of the many empty tables and tossed several rolled parchments onto it. The library was vacant with the exception of two robed men, both of them much too old to be of any help with the battle that raged outside the walls. Apparently, they'd been left to themselves.

"Can I help you with anything?" one of the men asked as he approached her.

Her first thought was to ignore him, but as she looked around the library, she quickly realized it would be hard for her to find what she was looking for on her own.

"Yes, actually. I'm looking for anything on the tattoo magic of the elves."

The man raised a brow in curiosity but didn't question her.

"I also need a quill, an empty vial for ink, some parchment, bandages, and a small metal container that I can burn something in."

"That's quite a list," the old man said. "You aren't planning on burning anything in here, are you? Many of these books are very old and could easily catch fire."

Jovanna stared at the man as if he were some sort of odd creature.

"Of course I'm going to burn something in here, you old fool. But I'm not going to be burning anything next to the books. Now go and get me what I need."

The man hesitated, but at the deadly gaze she settled on him, he quickly left. He returned a few minutes later with everything she requested. She unrolled one of the scrolls and saw the old man's eyes widen in shock when he realized that the scrolls were made of flesh and not parchment. He set the items on the table and left without a word.

Jovanna smirked at his reaction and continued working. She traced the outline of the tattoo onto a piece of parchment. Then, using the edge of the quill, she cut into the flesh along the outline of the tattoo that marked the patch of skin. She set the extra skin aside and put the tattooed portion into the metal bowl. Calling to the magic that was floating around her, she commanded it to heat the bottom of the bowl.

A burning smell began to fill the air. She sifted the charred skin in the bowl and was pleased to see the ink pooling at the bottom. Once the skin was completely burned, she poured the ink into the vial. She followed the same process for each of the rolled pieces of skin, four in all.

Once she had collected all of the ink, she looked at the items on the table and noticed that the man didn't bring her any books. She growled in frustration and got up. After several minutes of searching for one of the men, she gave up and started searching the rows of books herself. They were well organized, but most of them were covered with a thick layer of dust. She saw familiar titles from her days in the wizard city Palindrom, but many more titles that she did not know.

A Lineage of Kings.

Languid Poetry.

She walked a few aisles over and continued her search.

The History of Talvaard.

Tattoo Origins.

She stopped and pulled the book out, brushed the dust off the cover, and flipped through the pages. After a few minutes of scanning through the pages, she concluded the book would not be helpful. She placed it back on the shelf and continued looking.

Three shelves down she found another book. *The Tenth War.* She frowned, trying to remember where she'd heard the title before. She couldn't remember. She pulled the book out and started flipping through it. She carried it back to her table and sat down. It was a detailed account of the Tenth War, a time of bloody history in the kingdom of Talvaard. The narrator was part of the war and present for most of the fighting.

We never expected it to happen, she read. *The slaves had been so useful to that point, it hardly seemed like they would rebel. They were well treated and taken care of, so why would they rise against us? None of us knew the answer. We all were fearful, however. We had given them positions of trust, so they knew everything about us. They knew our secrets.*

It finally came to war. The slaves united behind one of their own. He was intelligent and charismatic. None of us were quite sure whose slave he had been, but that mattered little. He convinced the others, the few slaves who still trusted us and wanted peace, to turn aside from our kindness and to raid our cities. The first few raids were expected. We had assumed it would happen due to their anger. When the attacks didn't stop, that's when we knew it was much more serious than we had first believed.

The leader of the rebellious elves, who had named himself Tairu, mounted attack after attack on the undefended towns and villages.

Jovanna stopped reading. "Tairu?" she muttered. "It couldn't be the same …" the thought gave her pause. Was it possible that it was the same elf? Elves were long-lived compared to the humans, but how long-lived exactly? She calculated the years and shook her head. "He would have to be over a thousand years old," she said aloud. She kept reading.

The magical tattoos our wizards had given them quickly became a curse to us. They used them to slaughter us. Some of the elves had learned to alter the original purpose of the tattoos and they changed them into something destructive. They were able to blast through stone walls and deflect arrows with their skin.

Jovanna sat back in her chair. She didn't believe this was a coincidence. She'd lived among the elves for a few months and none of them had the stone skin tattoo. She'd never seen them blast through stone walls until she witnessed their march on the first walled city they had attacked. She turned the page and saw a symbol drawn on the top right. She'd seen it before. She closed her eyes and tried to remember where. It was recently. In the first city, the elves had attacked. When she saw Tairu.

She'd just killed a kid. She hadn't known he was a kid. He was dressed in armor and helping to defend the city from the elves. She had tried to break away from the rushing army, but she couldn't. She'd been forced into the city and had to make a decision. So she had killed the human guard. Shortly after, Tairu entered the city with a few personal guards.

She had drawn her sword and stalked toward him. She encountered his guards first. She slew them easily and swung her sword at Tairu, thinking to decapitate him. Her sword had merely clanged against his skin. She'd realized then that he had the stone skin tattoo, but his flesh was a normal color. It wasn't like the other elves whose skin had turned a grayish hue. She tossed the sword and their battle became one of magic.

Lightning bolts, waves of fire, and other magical attacks filled the air. Upon their first encounter, she had almost killed him. Fighting with him the second time led her to believe she'd only caught him off guard in their first battle, for he was very skilled at using his magical tattoos. They seemed evenly matched in power, neither one gaining an advantage.

If it weren't for several of his warriors joining the fray, she might have seen which of them was the better. She quickly became outnumbered and had to flee. During one of his attacks, he had come close enough that she could have landed a blow on him. Were she not focused on defending against his attack, she would have struck him bodily. She remembered that now. She had thought for a brief second of hitting him in the throat.

His throat. That's where she had seen the tattoo in the book. Jovanna opened her eyes. She looked at the symbol on the page again. Yes, she was sure of it now. The Tairu who incited a rebellion a thousand years ago was the same Tairu attacking people today.

"Where has he been for the last thousand years?"

She also wondered how he had lived that long. Elves were known for their ability to live a long time, but a thousand years was a stretch even for an elf. Many questions plagued her, but she pushed them from her mind. She'd come here with a purpose. Jovanna rolled her left pant leg up and set her ankle across the knee of her other leg. She placed the paper with the outline of the tattoo on her calve. Unsheathing a small dagger from her waist, she stabbed through the paper and into her flesh.

Her eye twitched from the sting, but she continued. She traced the blade along the outline on the paper, creating shallow scratches on her skin. Once she was finished, she removed the paper and eyed the shape. Blood seeped from the dagger marks, but not much. Taking the quill and the vial full of ink she'd removed from the skin, she dipped the quill in the vial and began filling the scratches with it.

As she worked, she could feel the magic working under her skin. The ink began to fuse with her blood, binding them together with a magical connection. Jovanna felt exhilarated. She always felt powerful when casting spells, but this was something entirely different. She could see the magic in the air, hovering over the tattoo as she applied the ink.

Once the vial was empty, she used the bandages the old man had brought to wrap the tattoo. Unrolling the next piece of skin, she followed the same process. She did that for all six of the tattoos she collected. She tattooed all of the designs on her legs. When she finished the last one, she stood up and stretched.

Her body thrummed with power. It raged within her, seeking an escape. How the elves managed to refrain from using the magic for so long, she didn't know. She felt compelled to use it right there, to unleash its power and destroy everything in her path. But she didn't.

She needed to test the magic. The elves tattooed themselves from head to toe with runes. They each had different effects, but they were all designed for war. The longer the elf kept from using the magic, the more powerful it became. She tried to imagine what the elders in the elven tribes felt like. All that power boiling under the surface, ready to be poured out.

Jovanna left her mess for the old men to clean up, but she grabbed the book and took it to the room she'd been given. She tossed it on the bed and made her way to the courtyard. The sounds of battle could be heard. The elves had attacked the walls every day since Garrick's departure. Arrows from both sides flew through the air. Blasts shook the ground as the elves continued to breach the walls with their explosive magic.

How would she get outside the walls to test the tattoos? Then she remembered the secret entry that Garrick had brought her through. Everyone was occupied with the fighting at the walls, so she doubted anyone would see her. She jogged to the door and paused in front of it. Once she opened it, she wouldn't be able to close it. It could only be opened and closed from the inside.

Jovanna didn't care. She pushed the door open and slipped out. Excitement welled up in her as she made her way around the castle toward the fighting. The magic clawed at her from the inside, trying desperately to get free. Her hands began to tremble involuntarily. She rounded the corner of the castle wall and entered the chaos. Elves were charging the wall. Arrows filled the sky and the humans were tossing large rocks from the wall. Some of them hit their mark and crushed the charging elves, blood splattering in every direction.

A few elves caught sight of her and ran toward her. Her heart was beating rapidly in her chest. Her hands continued to shake. The magic demanded to be loosed. It demanded to be used. Jovanna watched as the elves drew nearer, focusing on the one at the front. Time seemed to slow down. Every step he took seemed to take an eternity.

Her body raged against her mind. She flushed so hot

that she was cold, so cold that she was hot. Her flesh felt like it was on fire and steam began to waft from her clenched hands. She kept her focus on the lead elf.

Five steps.

The magic was almost uncontrollable.

Four steps.

She couldn't wait anymore.

Three steps.

It was going to kill her.

Two steps.

Flames leaped off her skin.

One step.

She exhaled and released the magic.

THE END OF BOOK THREE

ABOUT THE AUTHOR

Richard Fierce lives in Georgia with his wife and three step-daughters. He is the author of seven novels including Dragonsphere. Feel free to contact the author.

Email: Richard.Fierce@yahoo.com